JOHN B SPENCER

was born in west London, where he still lives with
his wife Lou and the youngest of their three sons.
This is his seventh novel.

A paperback original.

First Published in Great Britain in 1999 by
The Do-Not Press Ltd
16 The Woodlands
London SE13 6TY
www.thedonotpress.co.uk
email: thedonotpress@zoo.co.uk

ISBN 1 899344 50 0

British Library Cataloguing in Publication Data. A catalogue
record for this book is available from the British Library.

b   d   f   h   g   e   c   a

Printed and bound in Great Britain by
The Guernsey Press Co Ltd.

Stitch

JOHN B SPENCER

BLOODLINES

To Tom, Will and Syd.

Again... the activities and attitudes of the characters in this novel may be the author's concern, but they are not his responsibility.

Acknowledgements:
The usual crew... especially Jimmy B and William S. Also, Stephanie S, Jenny S, Pat I, Ann E, Micky B, Zöe A, Tom and Syd, Clare and Max, Terry R, Maggie R, Nene, Steve B, Martin S, John G, Brian T, and brother Ginge... thanks.

The CT Scan notice is – unbelievably – for real, but emanated from St Mary's Hospital, not Charing Cross. Sorry, Charing Cross. Special thanks to Dr Simon Stewart for keeping the brackets open.

chapter 1

'Come on, part-timers!'

1

Bobby-Boy and Charlie Paul at an outside table, Cordova's, Chiswick High Road, Saturday lunchtime crowd in, neither Bobby-Boy nor Charlie looking like they belonged, both wearing whatever... T-shirts, jeans, trainers. Should have been wearing chino shorts, three-button Ralph Lauren Polo tops, Timberland deck shoes, no socks.

Designer labels?

Who *gave* a fuck?

Both smoking Marlboro Lights – Charlie's packet – drawing disapproval despite they were seated outside, Bobby-Boy's word on non-smokers: Fuck 'em... bunch of chicken-shit pansies! Charlie Paul's word on pansies, 'That bloke in America who shot the President? Didn't he call himself a pansy?' Bobby-Boy, needing to think about that one, saying, 'Patsy, you dick-breath. It was Lee Harvey Oswald and he called himself a patsy.'

Bobby-Boy waiting on a pizza, American Hot, with pepperoni sausage, like they did across the road at Pizza Express. Charlie – why they had come to Cordova's – had ordered the all day breakfast, swore it was the best in Chiswick: egg, bacon, hash browns, sausage and tomato, mushrooms and baked beans extra. Bobby-Boy looking through the glass dividers, hoping to catch the waitress's eye, wondering how the fuck long they were going to have

9

to wait for the beers, two cold ones from the cooler cabinet, Peroni, Italian shit...

Charlie bending his ear about Toyah, how he hadn't seen her for a while, how was she keeping? Charlie, soft spot for Toyah, could never leave it alone, despite Bobby-Boy had made it clear he would take Charlie's head off at the shoulders, he even so much as thought about it. Bobby-Boy remembering what his old man had told him, the only piece of advice he had ever offered, apart from, 'Don't shit on your own door step.' Just watched *The Godfather* on television, fuck knows how many times that made, thought he was Marlon, saying, 'A beautiful woman is like a loaded gun. She is dangerous. Men will never behave rationally around a beautiful woman.' Bobby-Boy saying, at the time, 'Oh, do fuck off, Pop...'

Thinking, now, Too fucking right! Why he had made the biggest mistake of his life, married Toyah – Toyah the Destroyer – this, fifteen years ago, Toyah, four years younger than Bobby-Boy, now thirty-two, still drop dead beautiful. Bobby-Boy saying to her this morning, before they were dressed, still in the bedroom, Toyah wanting to know, how come they didn't do it any more? 'You want to know how come we don't do it any more? You never come on to me, never make any moves, and you're complaining we don't *do* it any more?' Holding up his hands, palms some nine inches apart, like he was showing Toyah the size of a fish he had caught, or – fat chance – the length of his dick, saying, not wanting another argument, not this time of the morning, 'What you have to understand is... you do this' – nodding towards his hands – 'then, I have to do this.' Moving his hands, palms the same distance apart, to the left. 'I'm not being judgmental. It's just how it is... cause and effect.'

Saying, now, to Charlie, 'Why don't you call round the house, you miss Toyah so much?'

Charlie thinking, Is he taking the piss?

Giving Bobby-Boy the new look he had been cultivating.

Picked it up from a war novel.

Vets back from 'The Nam'.

The thousand yard stare.

Bobby-Boy saying, 'The fuck you looking at me like that?'

Waitress arriving with the beer. Bobby-Boy looking up, smiling, saying, 'That's fine, love, we didn't want glasses.' The waitress saying, 'Did you want glasses?' Meaning: What kind of sheltered housing did this dip-shit just escape from? Bobby-Boy saying, 'Forget it, why don't you?' Bobby-Boy and Charlie watching her go back inside, take an order from a mother, three kids, just left of the door.

Charlie saying, 'If looks could kill.'

Kids all shouting at once.

Bobby-Boy saying, 'Well, fuck her.'

The mother saying, 'You'll get nothing at all if you don't sit down and *be* quiet!'

Her voice louder than the kids.

Bobby-Boy seeing where they got it from.

Charlie saying, 'You think it would be a good idea?'

'What?'

His attention still on the mother and her three brats.

Thinking, The brat and her three kids... more like.

'Toyah? You think it would be OK, I popped round?'

Felt almost sorry for the waitress.

Saying: 'I'd have you... you know that, don't you?'

'Oh, fuck off, Bobby-Boy.'

Then: 'It was your fucking idea.'

'You know what I mean.'

Bobby-Boy thinking: Do I really give a fuck? Toyah going weird on him, Bobby-Boy not sure if she was off sex in general or off him in particular. Then, this morning, out of the blue, 'How come we don't do it any more?' The fuck was she about? Toyah, taken to wearing a nightdress in bed, Bobby-Boy saying, 'Why are you hiding yourself? What is this?' Perfect figure, Toyah needed to cover herself up? Toyah saying, 'I don't feel comfortable. We're not teenagers any more.' Bobby-Boy thinking, Teenagers? *Teenagers*? The word 'teenager' past its sell-by date even when they *were* teenagers... at it all the time, back seat of Bobby-Boy's first decent set of wheels, Golf GTi, white finish. Bobby-Boy couldn't remember Toyah ever complaining. Then, when the Tina Turner song came out – 'Steamy Windows' – on the radio all the time, Bobby-Boy saying to Toyah, both of them laughing, 'Listen, they're playing our song.' Bobby-Boy remembering how Toyah had brought him off, one time, head buried in his lap, one hundred and five miles an hour, outside lane of the M2, heading for Margate, nearly wrote the fucker off, Bobby-Boy thinking, Way to go!

Toyah, now, saying, 'Reminds me of oysters.

'You know I can't stand oysters.'

Bobby-Boy thinking...

Fifteen years.

Sweet fucking Jesus!

The pizza and Charlie's fry-up arriving.

Too much hassle explaining to the waitress, Bobby-Boy and Charlie swapping plates after she was gone, Charlie waving his fingers in the air, saying, 'Fuck, these plates are hot!'

One dish waiting on the other.

Charlie's fry-up seen too much hot plate.

Save the waitress's legs.

Bobby-Boy checking her out...

Fuck all worth saving, there.

The table with the three brats, one of them crying, face full of Ben and Jerry ice cream, the mother saying, 'Harriet, oh, please *do* shut up!'

Charlie breaking his egg, looking for the yolk to soak into his toast, Bobby-Boy saying, 'Chance would be a fine thing.' Not sure if he was talking about Harriet shutting up or Charlie's yolk soaking into the toast. Taking his knife, cutting the American Hot into wedges – like he was slicing a gateaux – rolling up one of the wedges, from the outside in, putting the rolled wedge into his mouth.

Saying to Charlie, 'You looking at?'

Charlie saying, 'That how you eat pizza?'

Bobby-Boy, clearing his mouth, saying, 'You watch me do it, then, you say, "That how you eat pizza?" '

Making a gun with his index finger and thumb.

Pointing the finger at Charlie's head.

Saying, 'Boom.'

2

The selection of yoghurts available, Sophie Grace would often go into a catatonic state staring at the row upon row of them, her back to the cheese shelves, hands gripping the orange plastic handle of the shopping trolley.

Organic, bio, natural, thick and creamy, custard-style, Greek-style, with or without honey, raspberry, strawberry, gooseberry, blackberry and apple, fruits of the forest, rhubarb with crumble, banana with chocolate chip, cheesecake, mango, cherry, vanilla, all shapes and sizes, single cartons, two-packs, four-packs, special offer, one free every two you buy, family size economy packs.

Catatonia.

Past the point of making a rational decision.

Needing to make *a* decision.

Any decision.

Just to escape from aisle seven…

Sainsbury's.

Chiswick Branch.

Remembering how Jim used to come back to find her – knew where she would be – Jim already at the booze counter picking up his bottle of Sainsbury's own brand Finest Old Matured Scotch Whiskey, or, if a royalty cheque had arrived, a bottle of bonded Jack Daniel's, pretend he was Keith Richard, still delivering the chops, Fender Telecaster, hadn't touched it for ten years, not taken it out of the case, even, once the consultant had diagnosed multiple sclerosis. Jim saying, 'Hey, Sophie, I've lived more than most… we can handle this thing, right?' Sophie not believing a word of it… No regrets? Sophie thinking, Oh, Jim, this is me, Sophie, we don't have to pretend. The last few months of his life a living hell, Jim helpless, incontinent, worst of all, his mind still sharp as a button. Sophie grief-stricken, at the same time relieved and guilty when he finally died, the doctors shaking their heads, talking auto-fibrillation, muscular deterioration, spasm, his lungs no longer able to function, Sophie abiding by Jim's last coherent request, not allowing him to be taken into hospital, put on a ventilator, prolong his agony. Jim saying, 'What the fuck, Sophie,

13

we've been there, right?' 'Been there', as in lead guitarist, second division '60s Mod band, The Crunch: Italian suits, tab collars, chisel-toes... Cecil G, John Steven, Carnaby Street before it went to tat, tourists moved in, buy any shit, show the folks back home in Milwaukee, honourable brethren in Kyoto. Sophie still receiving royalties two years after his death, Jim's song, 'Maybe Tomorrow', covered by Tom Jones, kept resurfacing on various compilations, remembering Jim saying, when he was still able to laugh, 'You think of any easier way to make a living?'

Sophie aware of Jim's disappointment.

Just beneath the surface.

Never made it big-time.

Picturing him, now, appearing at the end of the supermarket aisle, taking a four-pack of yoghurt, any yoghurt, not even bothering to look, throwing it into Sophie's shopping trolley, saying, 'Wakey, wakey! Is there anybody home?' Reminding her that yoghurt used to be for health-freak nutters: the milkman leaving it on the door-step, third of a pint, red or white, in glass bottles... strawberry or vanilla, all you could get when they were kids. Sophie feeling old just thinking about it, wanting then, as now, to get back indoors, ten mil tab of Temazepam, Valium, Librium, whatever it took... the one time she had tried to cut back: sickness, diarrhoea, hallucinations, every morning, wake up, have a bath, then wait for the day to end. Blaming the '60s: uppers, downers, too much sulphate, blueys, brownies, whatever they stuck down their throats to make it through the night. Remembering Jim's regular gig, the Rainbow Rooms, Brighton – when The Crunch weren't on tour supporting some major league act, The Faces, The Who – Jim driving her down to Brighton on the back of his Vespa GS Scooter, later, them in the back of the band's Ford Transit, no windows... where she conceived the baby, the boy. Sweet seventeen, bringing shame on the family, the child born in the maternity wing of a remote convent hospital, north Devon, taken from Sophie's arms by the nuns, only a day old, given over for adoption, so much for the 'swinging' '60s.

Aurelie, their daughter, born two years later, Jim and Sophie married by this time – had to, they wanted a place together –

Registry Office, Hammersmith Town Hall. Jim's parents, Sophie's parents, all saying, 'Why don't you have a proper wedding... in a church?' None of them stepped inside a church since the last family christening, wedding, funeral. Jim saying, 'Fucking hypocrites, the lot of them,' not meaning it as harshly as it sounded. Aurelie, thirty now, divorced, living back with Sophie, Sophie not sure if that was a curse or a blessing. Aurelie home now, making cups of tea, looking after the builders – knocking through the bathroom and toilet, making the one room – plumbing, plastering, rewiring, sanding the floors, redecorating. Sophie couldn't believe the mess when that wall came down, Aurelie and Sophie having to use the kitchen sink downstairs to wash, pee – and, whatever – in the outside loo... pure hell.

Imagining what Jim would have made of it all: Jim with his pathological hatred of dustmen, milkmen and – especially – builders. Sophie saying to him, once, 'What about postmen? How come you don't hate postmen?' Jim saying, 'Are you crazy? Why should I hate postmen?' Jim on builders: 'Copy of the *Sun* in their back pocket, fat gut from all those nine o'clock fry-ups every morning, always moaning, making value judgments on how other people live. When's the last time this place saw a Hoover? State of the cooker, ten years of grease... all that kind of shit. What a fucking bunch of old women!' And: 'Reason Benidorm is full of chippies... all those hard man builders pissing their pants at the thought of going into a strange restaurant.' Sophie remembering one early afternoon in the Autumn, Jim in the back garden in his dressing gown, just back from a badly organised and gruelling seven week tour of Holland, Belgium and Germany. Builder, half-way up a ladder, next door, seeing Jim still in his dressing gown, two o'clock in the afternoon, muttering, 'All right for some.' Jim throwing windfall apples, Coxes Orange Pippin, shouting, 'Mind your own fucking business, you old tart!' Punctuating each syllable with an apple, the builder saying, 'Oi! That hurts!' Seven out of ten apples finding their mark...

The young kid, Robert, one of the builders back at the house, into '60s retro, awe-struck that this was where Jim Grace, *the* Jim Grace, actually used to live. Seen a framed photograph of the band on the kitchen wall, wanted to know everything there was to know about Jim and the band, said he had a mint copy of *Oceans Away*, the first of only two albums The Crunch ever made, cost him forty-five pounds at a collector's auction. Aurelie showing Robert the Fender Telecaster, happy to impress. Sophie, not interested, not wanting to discuss Jim with the kid... with anybody.

Still staring at the yoghurts.

Waiting for him to come along, rescue her.

Crying.

3

The start of all Bobby-Boy's real troubles, Wednesday, early afternoon, rain pissing down, weather just broken, kids back to school, second, third week of September? Three bedroom terraced house, Grove Park, five minutes walk from the riverside pubs at Kew Bridge. First floor master bedroom, bay window facing front, decor pastel blue, cream trim, rubberwood furniture with beech finish, on the double bed, duvet with matching pillows, white linen, falling green leaf pattern. One framed print on the wall facing the bed. Block of letters, the letters getting smaller towards the bottom. Bobby-Boy laughing, thinking, Eye test chart? Who the fuck would want a framed eye test chart on their bedroom wall? The two of them laying there every night, him saying, 'That's very good, now, the next line, can you tell me any of the letters on the next line?' His wife saying, 'A... F... H...? I think it's an H, or, is it an M?' Bobby-Boy, already been through the wardrobe, pulling drawers, one by one, from the dressing table, emptying them onto the bed...

Then, hearing the noise downstairs.

Front door slamming.

Low voices.

Girl giggling.

Bobby-Boy thinking, Fucking what, now?

From the bedroom door, seeing them down there in the hall, couldn't wait to get their clothes off, the man, wrong side of forty, the girl – she was a girl, not a woman – could have been his daughter. Any justice, way the two of them were going at it, they would never make it as far as upstairs to the bedroom.

Bobby-Boy thinking, Dirty fucker. Wife and two daughters packed off to some place hot, new term just starting, fuck the kids' education... should have been on the flight, too, according to Bobby-Boy's information: mini cab driver, not the one drove the family to Heathrow, mate of his, worked out of the same office in Fisher's Lane. The fucker – obvious, now – just along for the ride, wave goodbye from the observation deck, make sure they caught the flight. Bobby-Boy's contact saying – what the driver told him – the husband looked familiar, knew him from somewhere, something on the TV?

Bobby-Boy laughing.

Recognising the man.

Read the weather, early evening, after the news.

No idea what the fuck his name was...

The girl wearing pedal-pusher jeans, cut just below the knee, grey crushed velvet, weatherman showing his age, no idea how to get them off from round her tight little arse, her against the wall, head thrown back, him with his face buried in her neck, hands all over her, now, underneath her top, cupping her in his hands, same hands you saw every night waving around in front of a back-projection screen, map of the British Isles, Ireland, the coast of France – 'Temperatures will remain much the same as yesterday throughout the south-east, however, as you see, this cold front moving in across the Atlantic' – sucking on each nipple in turn, girl, mouth wide open, reaching between them, hand pushing into the top of his trousers, Bobby-Boy could have led the full England Squad, twenty-two players, manager, coach, trainers, faith healers, out past them, they wouldn't have noticed a fucking thing.

The girl saying, 'The bedroom, Gary, let's go upstairs.'

Bobby-Boy thinking, Oh, fuck, here we go.

The weatherman saying, 'Yvonne, my sweet darling.'

Bobby-Boy thinking, Yvonne? What kind of name was 'Yvonne,' young girl, couldn't be more than seventeen? Bobby-Boy had an aunt, dead, now, was called Yvonne. Bobby-Boy and his cousins, her two sons, when they were kids, grabbing hold of their bollocks, behind her back, laughing, saying, 'Yvonne? Then heave on this, darling!' Dropping the 'h'. Thought they were being *so* original.

Kids?

The fuck did they know?

At his aunt's funeral – ovarian cancer, the size of a football before the GP got round to referring her – the cousins, all in their late teens by now, reminiscing, the two sons at that age, too fucking stupid to let it show, even among their own... how devastated they were by their mother's death.

Bobby-Boy crossing the upstairs landing, keeping back from the balustrade, floor carpeted, making no sound: first door on his left, past the toilet and bathroom, Spice Girls posters, All Saints, Bart Simpson doll on the bed, PC on a desk, pile of *Smash Hits, Top of the Pops, TV Hits*, copies of the *Beano*, no way was he going to shag her in here, his daughter's bedroom. Bobby-Boy crossing to the window, view of the back garden, still pissing down outside. Immediately below the window a conservatory, glass and aluminium frame, through the glass, plants in pots, water feature, half-relief terracotta cherub spouting water over a pile of pebbles, green with moss, big yucca in one corner, spiked leaves – Bobby-Boy recognised the yucca. Toyah had bought him one, not that big, one birthday, said, 'Here, give yourself an interest in life, keep this alive.' The yucca dead in two months... over-watering. Bobby-Boy checking the drop, the roof of the conservatory, thinking, No way. Not even if push did come to shove.

The two of them on the stairs, now, coming up slowly, not wanting to break apart, lose the moment. Yvonne saying, no more than a whisper, 'I've got some if you haven't.' Gary, the weatherman, giggling – forty-plus years old and giggling like a fucking school-girl, Bobby-Boy thinking, Christ preserve us! – Gary saying, 'Come prepared, then, did we?'

Yvonne saying, 'It didn't take a mind-reader.'

Bobby-Boy behind the half open door of the kid's bedroom, closing it, they might have heard, eyeball to eyeball with Shaznay, the black All Saint, poster his side of the door, could see the top of

18

the hall stairs through the crack, wondering what the fuck Charlie had been up to not noticing anything... sent him round four times, usual scam, set the alarm off, get the neighbours used to the racket, assume the system is playing up, not bother calling the police – who the fuck called the police for an alarm, anyway? Those Neighbourhood Watch stickers, 'We Beat Crime Together', you had to laugh. This year's model, what they were all buying, Yale High Security Alarm, two hundred quid, Sainsbury's Homebase – or, money to burn, Mark IV Trifid, one-o-five decibel siren, fit-inducing strobe, a snip at three and a half grand – the Yale High Security no problem, once inside, even with – and how many bothered? – cable protector fitted, trigger the alarm when the power source cut. Bobby-Boy blaming himself, too. Elementary precaution, check the kitchen, first: fresh milk, butter, in the fridge, loaf of bread on the table, breakfast plates in the sink, it didn't take a Stephen Hawking.

Dumping his hold-all, tools, tyre lever on the kitchen table.

Noticing the Four Slot Chrome Dualit Toaster on the work surface by the sink, nothing else...

One hundred and seventy pounds of anybody's money.

Was he fucking stupid or what?

Not wanting to answer that one.

The couple stumbling on the final stair, losing their balance, then, stretched out on the landing carpet, Yvonne saying, 'Wait,' rolling away from the weatherman, pulling off the pedal-pushers, Gary on his knees, trousers and boxer shorts round his ankles, pealing on a condom, pink ribbed tickler, Bobby-Boy willing them to move on past to the master bedroom, knowing it was already too late for that. The two of them groaning in unison as Gary drove between her legs, Yvonne scissoring her ankles above his back, hands spread, nails digging into his backside, Gary going, 'Oh, Christ, Yvonne!' Banging his head against the half-open bedroom door, head thrown back, coming, already, staring up at Bobby-Boy standing there in his daughter's room...

Bobby-Boy saying, 'Oh, fuck it!'

Stepping over them.

Down the stairs.

Picking up his hold-all from the kitchen table.

Deciding against the Dualit.

Back in the hall, Gary, the weatherman, waiting. Bobby-Boy saying to him, 'You don't want to do this, Gary.' Gary saying, 'Like fuck I want to do this!'

Top of the stairs, leaning over the balustrade, Yvonne screaming, 'You fucking bastard pervert!'

Then: 'Voyeuristic wanker!'

Naked from the waist down...

Gorgeous legs.

Bobby-Boy reaching into the hold-all for his tyre lever, thinking, 'Nah,' making a fist, fore-arm horizontal, level with his shoulder, the way an archer would, pulling back the bow-string of his long bow, punching Gary hard in the face. Gary saying, 'Oh,' both hands to his nose, blood gushing between his fingers. Bobby-Boy thinking, Chances are, nobody would be seeing Gary read the weather next few days.

Shouldering past Gary.

Out the front door.

4

'Jesus, Winston!'

Winston's tongue, the *stud* in Winston's tongue.

Toyah saying, 'I am about to go crazy.' The 'crazy' as three syllables... *ker-ray-zee*. Pulling at her own hair, eyes watering, legs spread, Winston's head down there, back exposed, his shoulders, the wings of an American bald eagle, writhing sidewinder grasped in the eagle's talons, a background of swirling flame, a kaleidoscope of snow-capped mountain peaks, skulls, somewhere in there a Harley Davidson chopper, heraldic scroll with the words: FUCK WITH ME! Winston telling Toyah the tattoo was a backpiece, one day of consultation, sketches, three days to complete, Biker Jim's, *the* tattoo artist, people came to him from all over, worked out of a basement studio, just off the green, Ealing Broadway. Toyah wanting to know how much it had hurt – this, the first time they were together. Winston unzipping his jeans, gold ring through his prick, laughing, saying, 'Not as much as this.' Then: 'You never heard of a Prince Albert?' Telling Toyah it was called a Prince Albert on account of Queen Victoria's old man, the Prince Regent, having a ring through *his* prick to avoid getting a hard-on, tight trousers, public engagement, the whole thing too embarrassing to even think about. Toyah, not sure what to believe, grabbing Winston's prick, saying, 'So, how come it doesn't work for you?' Winston, teasing, pulling back, not through with his lecture, saying, 'Those gold earrings sailors used to wear? That was to pay for their funeral, make sure they went out in style.' Toyah counting the gold rings: six in one ear – the left – nostril, tongue, two in Winston's right nipple, the one through his prick, saying, 'What is it you're expecting... a state funeral?'

Winston, now, bringing her off.

Toyah out of control.

Screaming.

Thinking, Fuck the neighbours.

5

Kew Bridge Road solid, Kew Bridge into Richmond, what's new... Bobby-Boy and Charlie in the Beamer, 328i 3 Series, S-reg, black finish, Charlie, first time he saw the motor, saying to Bobby-Boy, 'Fuck you can afford wheels like this?' Bobby-Boy saying, 'Employing morons like you, Charlie, work for nothing.' Charlie laughing, seeing it as a big joke. Bobby-Boy showing Charlie all the toys for boys: tyre pressure sensors, sat-nav, rain-sensitive wipers, 'waterfall' instrument panel illumination, DSC. Bobby-Boy saying, 'DSC... dynamic stability control, you couldn't write this fucker off if you wanted to... drive like a prat, DSC takes control of the brakes and throttle. Running out of road is no longer an option.' Charlie passing on 'waterfall' illumination, showing interest, saying, 'What the fuck is 'sat-nav'?' Bobby-Boy saying, 'Satellite navigation. Tells you where you are, any time, day or night.'

Charlie saying, 'Very handy, you happen to be lost in the middle of the Sahara.'

Then: 'You're sounding like an anorak, Bobby-Boy.'

Bobby-Boy thinking, Hired help getting stroppy.

That would not do.

Would not do at all…

Saying, 'Fuck right off, will you, Charlie.'

Charlie Paul, two-fisted drinker, fuck-wit and first time loser, started out with Bobby-Boy, bit of this, bit of that, Bobby-Boy bunging him the odd tenner, keep him happy, he started whinging. One thing Charlie was always good for… whinging. Bobby-Boy at that time having a scene with a local primary school teacher, Adriana. Charlie Paul, porter at the same school, Hogarth Junior, making up his money running tobacco between Calais and Dover at the weekend, gave up the portering job after the school secretary called him into her office, told Charlie that from now on he was to be known as the Building Facilities Manager, the conversation going like this:

'Same hours?'

'Yes.'

'More money?'

'No.'

Charlie saying, 'Then, fuck you, I don't need the responsibility.'

Bobby-Boy explaining: 'It meant nothing, Charlie. It's just how it works. You remember Domestic Science, Home Economics, all that crap? Well, now, it's called Food and Textiles Technology, cooking and sewing to you and me, right? You go for a job interview, it's not the Personnel Department you want, it's Human Resources. You imagine the wankers come up with this shit? Rodent Operatives… oh, please!'

Charlie saying now, Kew Gardens on the right, the green, Bobby-Boy waiting to filter right towards Richmond, inside lane moving faster, bearing left at the lights, South Circular, heading for Mortlake: 'As it happens, I couldn't see too much wrong with your last motor.'

Bobby-Boy sighing.

Shaking his head.

Saying, 'Gear ratio was crap. Too big a gap between second and third. Changing down, no way could you slow down using the gears, not without kangarooing all over the fucking road, leave your gear-box in the rear-view mirror.' Then, thinking, the fuck am I bothering with this? Dick-breath is actually comparing a Passat – a fucking Volkswagen! – with a 3 Series BMW, saying, 'You truly amaze me, sometimes, Charlie, you really do.'

Coming up to Richmond.

The roundabout.

Slowing for the red, Bobby-Boy now thinking about Adriana, the school teacher, all the cafés along Chiswick High Road, seats outside, watch the world go by, perfect for pulling on a sunny afternoon... asking Adriana, over a *café latte*, first time they met, Bobby-Boy having trouble believing she was a teacher – wasn't boring, wasn't moaning – saying, 'So, what is it you teach, Adriana?'

Adriana saying, 'Bastards.'

Sharp as a button.

Body to die for...

No objection to the taste of oysters, either.

Living in San Francisco now, with a marine biologist.

Hearing the car horn.

The second the lights changed, car behind – rep's motor, blue Ford Mondeo, jacket on a hanger in the back – sounding his horn. Bobby-Boy applying the hand-brake, getting out of the BMW, Charlie leaning across, saying, 'You need help?' Bobby-Boy saying, over his shoulder, 'You must be fucking joking.' Coming up to the driver's side of the Mondeo, other drivers leaning on their horns now, Bobby-Boy not giving a fuck, making a winding motion with his hand, the driver, eyes front, hands gripping the steering wheel, not moving...

Not about to wind down his window, either.

No way.

Bobby-Boy saying, through the glass, leaning down, 'I am truly sorry if I have just ruined the whole of the rest of your life, wasting one second of your precious time like that... perhaps you would care to step out of the car, we can discuss it further?'

Driver still not moving.

Bobby-Boy thinking, Fuck it!

Back in the BMW.

Beating the lights on the red.

6

Robert unable to believe he was actually doing this.

Him, nineteen.

Aurelie, thirty.

Married.

Bus stop, Acton High Street, opposite the Tesco Supermarket, waiting for an E3, football training, Gunnersbury Park, the bathroom conversion finished last Friday, missing Aurelie, already… it had to be love.

Calling her on the mobile.

Ericsson.

Hearing the ringing tone.

Praying it wouldn't be Mrs Grace who answered.

Hearing Aurelie's sleepy voice.

Saying: 'I woke you up.'

Aurelie saying, 'It's ten-thirty on a Sunday morning, what would you expect?'

Then: 'Who is this?'

'Robert.'

'Robert?'

Then: 'Oh, Robert.'

Robert saying, 'I was wondering if you would like to go out?'

Aurelie saying, '"Out"? What do you mean, "out"?'

'You know… pictures, a drink somewhere.'

Remembering the extra twenty-five notes Bobby-Boy had given him last night, Robert in the Roebuck, Bobby-Boy passing through, saying, 'A token of my appreciation. Don't spend it all at once.'

Robert saying now, 'We could go for a meal.'

'A meal?'

'Do you like Indian? Or Chinese, maybe?'

Aurelie saying, 'Oh, Robert, you simpleton. Why don't you just come on over? What you want to do to me, you can't do when we're "out"?'

An E3 appearing in the distance.

At the junction with Acton Lane.

The Town Hall.

Robert, mouth open… no words coming out.

Aurelie saying, 'You still there?'

Robert: 'My bus is coming.'

Aurelie: 'Give me your number. I'll call you when my mother's going to be out.'

Robert giving his number.

Pressing cancel.

The E3 pulling up, doors sliding open.

Robert leaving his kit…

Boots, pads, shirt, shorts, towel.

All there in a hold-all on the pavement.

7

Green Carnation, Victoria Place, paved alley – arts and crafts shop, Polish delicatessen, antiquarian book shop, that kind of shit – off George Street, Richmond. Bobby-Boy made his peace with Winston, Winston saying, when they came through the door, dragging the noise of the traffic with them, 'Fuck you been?' Patrick, red velvet waistcoat, white shirt, dark bow-tie, taking their order, Bobby-Boy reaching for his wallet, Patrick pouring the drinks: same again, juice, for Winston, Bobby-Boy and Charlie on lager top, Grolsch Export. Bobby-Boy, polite conversation, humour Winston, only half-an-hour late, for fuck's sake, observing that he had never – ever – come across another white bloke, the name of Winston. Charlie Paul saying, 'Mate of mine had a dog called Winston… Labrador, but he was black, too.'

Bobby-Boy saying, 'You?'

Then: 'Mates?'

Winston, head shaved and waxed, black studded leather, crisp white T-shirt, jeans, leopard-skin trainers, Vans, direct mail order from Japan, cost an arm and a leg… bicycle or motorcycle security chain, two inch links, resist a hack-saw blade, hanging loose around his neck, the lock itself and the sister connection swinging free, waist-height. Winston, no bicycle, no motorcycle, no car, either: travelled everywhere by mini cab, local firm, speed-dialled them on the mobile.

Winston saying, 'You boys.'

Bobby-Boy saying, 'What must your old lady have been thinking about, name like Winston?'

Charlie saying, 'Who was she thinking about, more like?'

Bobby-Boy saying to Patrick, 'Did you ever hear of a white geezer called Winston, Patrick?'

Patrick saying, 'Winston Churchill?'

All of them looking at Patrick.

Winston saying, 'Shows you, Bobby-Boy, you can figure it out all you want, still get fucked,' thinking, Cut Bobby-Boy some slack, nailing his old lady to the mattress last six months, regular basis, least he could do. Now, Charlie Paul – fat, mouthy, Charlie 'Shit for Brains' Paul – that was a different matter… pictured lifting him off the floor by his head, squeezing till his skull popped.

Mate of mine had a dog called Winston.

Very close, Charlie.

Very close, indeed.

Bobby-Boy saying to Patrick, 'Don't you have somebody down the other end needs serving?'

Patrick taking the hint.

Moving away.

Charlie saying, 'We were Muslims, wouldn't be in here right now… wouldn't be allowed. Drinking, dancing, music, going to the flicks, watch a video – none of that.'

Bobby-Boy saying, 'Fucking staff, nowadays… attitude, wherever you look.'

Charlie saying, off on one, 'Floggings, amputations and executions… only entertainment they got. Down the sports stadium, take the wife and kids, packet of popcorn, way to spend your Sunday afternoon, right?'

Then: 'And the women – not allowed any education, hardly allowed out of the house, even.'

And: 'There's one works behind the counter in the Chiswick Post Office, wears one of those grey things they all wear, all you can see is the eyes.'

Patrick calling, the length of the bar, 'It's called a *bukka*.'

'What?'

26

'What they wear.'

Bobby-Boy saying, 'Shut the fuck up, will you, Charlie.'

Winston, remembering what Bobby-Boy had said about Charlie, So thick he thought Shrove Tuesday was on a Monday, saying, 'I'd be up for that.'

'Up for what.'

'Contribution... your air fare. Muslims fascinate you so much, you should fuck off, join them.'

'Risk having my hands chopped off?'

'Worse things could happen, Charlie.'

Bobby-Boy saying to Winston, 'Vintage guitars... what do you know?'

Winston saying, 'What do you want to know?'

'Fender Telecaster, 1962, natural wood finish, no customisation, original case, how much?'

'Good nick?'

'So I'm told.'

'Authentication?'

'Don't be daft.'

'It would pay you to look... Japanese market, anything between three and five grand.'

'You up for it?'

'Take it off you for two.'

'Fuck off.'

'Suit yourself.'

Charlie saying: 'Hardly cause for complaint, Bobby-Boy, two big ones for an afternoon's work.'

Then, to Winston: 'That one through your tongue, does that hurt?'

The gold ring.

Winston thinking of Toyah.

Her laying in the bath – she told him this – fingering herself beneath the surface of the water, her wedding ring, the feel of it reminding her of Winston.

Does it hurt?

Wondering how far they would take it.

Toyah and Winston.

27

The S and M.

Picturing Charlie and Bobby-Boy, their faces, he wanged out his prick on the bar stool, said, Not as much as this.

Bobby-Boy saying to Charlie, 'Fuck you on?'

Then...

Second time.

As many minutes.

'Shut the fuck up, will you, Charlie.'

chapter two

'Man on!'

1

Sophie hated it the way Aurelie paraded around the house with nothing on, Aurelie saying she wasn't used to the luxury of central heating – the first floor flat she had shared with her husband, Marcus, terraced house, Shepherd's Bush, single bar electric fire in every room, landlord making a fortune from the rigged meter, saying to Marcus, the one time he had complained – spineless bastard – 'This I am doing for *my* family, Mr Goodyear, not for *your* family.' Sophie saying to Aurelie, about her nakedness, 'It's hardly as if you had anything worth writing home about.' Aurelie saying, 'It's a generational thing, mother.' Aurelie, five foot nothing, narrow shoulders, breasts non-existent, proscribed by the areola of her nipples, boyish hips…a sparrow, like her father. Sophie often wondering, If she had had children with Marcus, would she have rounded out, become more of a woman?

Less of a slut.

Marcus now long gone.

Had enough of Aurelie's tantrums, his last word to Sophie on the subject, after she had rung the flat, stuck her nose in where it wasn't wanted – Jim dead only a year and now this – 'Your daughter, Mrs Grace…' – always 'Mrs Grace', never 'Sophie' – 'With your daughter, it's that time of the month every day of the month.'

Meaning: Aurelie was an irritable, short-tempered, self-serving bitch.

Sophie thinking, Tell me about it, Marcus.

Saying, 'Well, I know she can be difficult.'

Marcus saying, 'Difficult!'

Sophie saying, 'It hasn't been easy… her father…'

'I was fond of your husband, Mrs Grace. It was a terrible tragedy. But, I don't see how that changes anything.'

Jim fighting for breath.

The fear in his eyes…

Already gone to another place.

A place where Sophie could not be with him.

Sophie saying to Marcus, 'How could you know?'

Marcus saying, 'I'm sorry.'

'I don't doubt that, Marcus. I don't doubt that at all.'

Thinking, What difference did it make, Marcus being sorry?

What difference did it make, *anybody* being sorry?

Jim's hand circling her wrist.

The doctor saying, 'We'll have to move this, now.'

Sophie saying, 'Leave it! Leave it where it is!'

Sitting by the bed while Jim's hand grew cold.

Still circling her wrist.

Not crying.

Not yet.

Sophie still surprised – not hurt – by Jim's last word:

'Mother.'

Then the tears, when they did come, not, at first, for Jim, but for their own son abandoned at birth, given over to the nuns, barely a day old.

Wailing.

Marcus saying, over the telephone, 'You're a fine woman, Mrs Grace.'

Sophie saying, 'How little you know.'

The last words she spoke to him.

Thinking, What a pity.

Her daughter might have done a lot worse.

Probably, still would.

Aurelie on the settee in the living room now, *Animal Hospital*, Rolf Harris, on the television, Aurelie clutching a cushion to her breast, just out of the shower, cigarette burning in the ashtray, Aurelie knowing how much Sophie hated her smoking in the house, Sophie saying, 'Do you have to do that?' Aurelie, not looking up from the television screen – animals, pets, cats in particular, the only thing she ever got animated about – saying, 'When's dinner?'

2

Bobby-Boy had ordered chicken *fajitas*, jug of margaritas, crushed ice, the Navajo Bar, strip of restaurants and shops in an otherwise residential area, Salford Avenue, could see the front of the house from where he sat at a window table. Four o'clock, the place almost empty, waiter making it clear he hoped Bobby-Boy wasn't going to take his time, give the staff a breather before the after-work happy hour, Bobby-Boy thinking, You don't like the job, fuck off and do something else… Remembering the girl from last night, Club 67, whole place heaving. 'Day Tripper', The Beatles, on the sound system – *She was a day tripper, Sunday driver, yeah!* – Bobby-Boy up close to the girl's ear, explaining about *big teaser*, how what it really meant was *prick teaser*. The girl wanting to know, how come Bobby-Boy knew so much about The Beatles, was he a geriatric, or what? Telling Bobby-Boy she was an actress, knew Kate Winslet *and* Natascha McElhone. Bobby-Boy passing on Natascha McElhone, saying he's seen *Titanic* – but only the once. The girl telling Bobby-Boy she had an important audition in the morning, saying, 'I need to be home by ten-thirty.'

Bobby-Boy saying: 'I'm dancing as fast as I can.'

Thinking now, 'Humourless bitch.'

Seeing a woman coming out of the house.

Attractive.

Pushing fifty.

Passing the restaurant on the other pavement.

Bobby-Boy knowing, already, there were two women living in the house; the other, younger, the older woman's daughter. Neither of them working, keeping regular hours away from the house – could be a problem unless Bobby-Boy went in at night, broke one of his own golden rules... times he had said to Charlie, You know the house is occupied, just walk away. It isn't worth the grief. Hoping, now, watching the place, to clock some routine, some – Fuck! Was he actually using these words? – window of opportunity. He would need only fifteen minutes in there, no alarms, solid hedgerow obscuring the downstairs bay windows, concealing his access. Knew exactly what he was going in for, where it was – behind the clothes, wardrobe, upstairs master bedroom – thanks to Robert and his long chats with the daughter.

Robert saying to Bobby-Boy, 'Wouldn't mind giving *that* one, I don't mind telling you.'

Bobby-Boy saying, 'You surprise me.'

Then: 'You really do.'

Robert not getting it.

The irony.

Bobby-Boy thinking, Thick fucking bastard.

Waiter arriving with the *fajitas*, the chicken rich brown, sizzling, chunks of green pepper, mushrooms, side plate of steamed corn tortillas, Bobby-Boy telling Toyah, once, first time they had eaten Mexican, 'Third World version of Peking Duck.' The waiter sliding a saucer with the bill face down onto the table next to the tortillas.

Bobby-Boy saying, 'I ask for that?'

The waiter saying, 'I just thought...'

Bobby-Boy saying, 'You know what thought did, don't you, sunshine?' Something his old lady was always saying to him... never did work out what it meant. Remembering the one his old man used to come out with: 'To the woods! To the woods!' Then, in a high pitched voice, 'I'll tell the vicar.' Normal voice: 'I *am* the vicar.' His old man laughing himself into a coughing fit ever time over that one... Bobby-Boy well into his teens before he finally got it. Crumpling the bill, placing it in the waiter's hand, closing the waiter's fist around the bill.

Saying, 'I'll let you know.'

Upending his glass, twirling it in the salt dish, righting the glass, pouring another margarita, his third, the jug still half full.

Sipping the drink, watching the house, picturing the daughter in there alone, wondering what she was doing... hardly ever seemed to leave the house. Then, thinking about Toyah, last night, after he got back from the club, still pissed off with the bird, the way she gave him the heave-ho. *Prick teaser? Sunday Driver?* The fuck she think she was? Toyah coming on to him, must have been some rumpy-pumpy on the box, always got her going... always used to, anyway.

Saying: 'Squeeze.'

Then: 'Harder.'

Bobby-Boy thinking, Has to be on drugs.

Toyah, sharp intake of breath, saying again, 'Harder!'

Bobby-Boy, Toyah's nipple between his thumb and forefinger, saying, 'Doesn't that hurt?'

Toyah saying, 'What do you think?'

Then: 'You just don't get it, do you, Bobby-Boy?'

Then...

Turning away.

'Go to sleep, why don't you?'

A canary yellow Vauxhall Cavalier pulling up across the road, pumping exhaust fumes, bent MOT written all over, parking in front of the house. The driver getting out, locking the door – why the fuck bother, a Vauxhall Cavalier? – going up the garden path, ringing the bell. The younger woman opening the door, the two of them all over each other, couldn't wait to get straight to it, door closing behind them.

Bobby-Boy placing a tortilla on his plate, careful not to crease it. Adding chicken, green pepper, mushroom, not too much, the trick being not to overload the tortilla. Rolling the tortilla carefully...

Taking a bite.

Thinking: Robert, you sly old bastard, you.

3

Toyah thinking, What if?

What if I did leave Bobby-Boy?

Would the sky fall in?

Would I turn to stone?

Or, salt?

Who was it, turned to salt in the Bible?

Looked round when they shouldn't?

Weird book.

The Bible.

You believe that…

Bobby-Boy saying, this morning, 'Tattoo? You want a tattoo?'

Then: 'You're thirty-two fucking years old, Toyah. You want a tattoo. You think it's going to make you look younger?'

Younger.

Toyah remembering the two of them in the lift, Toyah still living in South Acton Estate, eleventh floor, Bobby-Boy always stopping the lift between the ninth and tenth, this *after* they had been at it in the back of Bobby-Boy's motor, the white Golf… Ten minutes later, Toyah's mum offering Bobby-Boy a cup of tea, coffee, saying, 'How was the film?' Didn't matter where they had been, it was always, 'How was the film?'

Bobby-Boy saying, 'Bit slow.'

Toyah saying, 'Don't think you would have liked it.'

Feeling Bobby-Boy dribbling down her thigh.

The two of them exchanging glances.

Toyah this morning, pushing down the plunger on the cafetière, imagining it was a detonator, blowing Bobby-Boy to kingdom come. Saying, 'I'm not talking Painted Lady… turning into some circus freak.'

'I should be so grateful.'

Pouring his coffee.

Leaving Toyah to pour her own.

'Just something small at the base of the spine.'

Bobby-Boy saying, 'What is the fucking point?'

Toyah saying, 'The coccyx.'

Bobby-Boy looking up from his coffee.

Saying, 'Coccyx?'

Then: 'Where the fuck you pick up a word like "coccyx"?'

Toyah saying nothing.

Bobby-Boy saying, 'Tell you what… you can spell coccyx,

34

have the fucking tattoo.'

Winston running his hand down Toyah's spine, reaching the cleft, saying, 'This is where your tail used to be.' Saying the word, coccyx. Toyah never heard it before, saying to Winston, 'Would you like it, I got a tattoo there, just for you?'

Then: 'What kind of tattoo?'

Winston saying, 'Surprise me.'

Soon as he'd gone, Toyah looking up the word in a dictionary.

Now, not sure if she should dare.

Thinking, Fuck it!

Saying, 'C-O-C-C-Y-X.'

Bobby-Boy, no idea if she had it right, or not.

4

According to Winston, all his big problems in life started on his tenth birthday, June 4th, 1975, when his parents told him, 'We decided we would tell you on your tenth birthday.' Winston saying now, 'Imagine – being told something like that on your tenth birthday.' Frank and Penny Capaldi, his adoptive parents, buying him a special birthday present: Scalextric Racing Car Set, Winston saying to Bobby-Boy and Charlie Paul, he swore that was the reason he had never given a flying fuck about motors – by association – never had the least desire to drive one or to own one. Telling Bobby-Boy and Charlie all this in McDonald's, Richmond High Street, frontage the same as when it was an expensive family-run Swiss restaurant, Vacheras – even Ronald McDonald didn't mess with Richmond money – Winston saying, 'Rally cars, right? BMW and a Porsche. Not even fucking Formula One.' Bobby-Boy and Charlie both quarter-pounders with cheese; Winston, a Big Mac; side order of fries apiece; Triple Shakes, Winston and Charlie, banana, Bobby-Boy, chocolate… Winston saying, 'Frank, he's telling me it's the rally cars that sort out the men from the boys, any fool can race a Formula One without rolling it – where's the skill in that? I'm thinking, The fuck do you know? You're not even my old man!' Two weeks later, Winston up before the beak, Horseferry Lane Magistrates Court, Juvenile Offenders Sessions.

Aggravated assault.

Cricket bat.

A kid in Winston's class had called him a bastard.

The kid requiring sixteen stitches in his head, kept in under observation overnight, emergency ward, Ducane Road Hospital, suspected concussion.

That time, Winston got off lightly.

Extenuating circumstances.

Six months juvenile remand, suspended, pending psychiatric evaluation. When the psychiatric report came through it was full of: 'associative trauma', 'over-reactive emotive response', 'temporary behavioural dysfunction…'

Shit like that.

Bobby-Boy thinking, Temporary?

Saying, 'Psychiatrists, right? Fuck do they know?'

Charlie Paul saying, 'Let me get this straight: what they're talking about, right, is one ten-year-old kid whacking another ten year old kid round the head with a cricket bat?'

Next time, Winston wasn't so lucky.

His legal aid telling him, 'You have to dress for the part… don't say I didn't warn you.' Frank and Penny in the public gallery wringing their hands. Winston, hair spiked up with Brylcreem, ring through the nose, bondage collar, ripped jeans, steel toe-capped DMs, gobbing from the dock when the judge passed sentence. In the holding cell, earlier, with Frank and Penny, saying to the solicitor, 'Why don't you just fuck right off!' Fourteen years old. 1979. The year Sid Vicious died at a party in New York City, heroin overdose, fluid on the lungs, out on $50,000 bail, accused of stabbing his girlfriend to death, Nancy Spungen.

Twenty-four months.

Haversham Juvenile Correctional Centre.

New Tory Party initiative…

Short, sharp shock.

Hop picking and physical exercise.

This time, the weapon a crow-bar.

Frank and Penny still where they had always lived, ground floor flat, neglected garden, opposite the Scrubs, Wood Lane.

36

Frank telling Winston, the day after he came home from the Correctional Centre, Penny was dying, breast cancer, mestasis, nothing the doctors could do but arrange for a Macmillan Nurse to call daily – 'Angel of fucking Death,' Frank called her – regulate the intravenous dosage of diamorphine. Two months after Penny was gone, Winston came home Saturday night, brain-dead on export lager, sulphate and 'ludes, found Frank in the bath, wrists slashed with a razor, one of Winston's, Wilkinson Sword – Winston often wondering why he should have noticed something like that – Frank's head half-submerged, mouth open in surprise, his pathetic little prick bobbing on the surface of the blood-red water.

After the funeral, Winston moved in with his Aunt Anastasia, Penny's older sister, a spinster, in Ealing.

Gave up drugs.

Took up body-building.

Shaved his head.

Got his first tattoo...

Lizard, left buttock.

Biker Jim telling Winston, 'You're safe with a lizard, something you can build on.'

Charlie Paul, finished his quarter-pounder with cheese, blowing his nose in a table napkin, screwing up the napkin, tossing it on his tray.

Bobby-Boy saying, 'That's fucking disgusting.'

Charlie saying, to Winston: 'Did you ever bite anybody's ear off?'

Bobby-Boy saying, 'Jesus fucking Christ!'

Charlie saying, 'It was Frank Tyson started all that, that comeback fight when he got out of jail, who was it, he took a lump out of his ear?'

Bobby-Boy saying, 'You get home, Charlie, better start putting labels on everything. Another couple of years and it will be too late. You won't remember fuck all.'

'I don't get you?'

'Think about it.'

Winston saying, 'Evander Holyfield.'

Charlie saying, 'That's right, Evander Holyfield... and there was that rugby player, before that. What was *his* name?'

Winston saying, 'Fuck I should know about rugby.'

Charlie, saying, 'Every Saturday night, now, after the clubs turn out, emergency ward full of them, lads with half an ear missing. Very nasty, the human bite. Doctor's consider it a worrying trend. Not easy, sewing an ear back on... very complicated organ.'

Then: 'You ask me, sport has a lot to answer for... forget all that violent films on the television.'

Bobby-Boy saying to Winston: 'Robert? Him shagging the daughter. You think that will be a problem?'

Winston saying, 'Not my problem, Bobby-Boy.'

Then: 'You want I should put the frights on him?'

'Nothing drastic.'

Winston saying, 'Trust me, Bobby-Boy.'

5

'You never did this before, did you?'

'Course I did.'

Robert, big.

Bigger than Marcus.

Aurelie saying, 'Well, aren't you the one.'

Thinking: Any woman says size doesn't count, never had a proper seeing to.

Mind you...

Robert, all over in seconds.

Looking into Aurelie's face.

Aurelie saying, 'Way to go, yet, kid.'

Robert, puzzled, saying, 'What do I do?'

Aurelie: 'First we get you motivated.'

Robert horrified.

Aurelie sliding down his chest, her tongue leaving a trail of saliva, taking him into her mouth. Robert relieved – not strong enough a word – that he had bothered to wash himself down there before coming over. For no reason that he could imagine, thinking of the Sunday morning game, his team mates shouting, 'Skills! Skills!' when he passed a man or put in a good cross.

Aurelie releasing his prick from her mouth.

Saying, 'OK, big boy, now where were we?'

6

David coming back into her life was a complication that Sophie did not need. Outside Marks & Spencer, Chiswick High Road, Sophie annoyed that the *Big Issue* vendor was not in his usual place – she had wanted to buy the special edition, edited by Damien Hirst – the greengrocer, pavement stall, been there years, his big joke in the eighties, 'You need a Rock Hudson, luv?' Meaning, 'carrier', as in 'carrier bag', this Friday's litany, 'Sweetcorn! Four for a pound! You can't ask fairer than that,' Sophie kicking herself, should have known better, just bought two in Marks & Spencer for 69p each, David standing in front of her on the pavement saying, 'Sophie?'

Almost twenty years.

Both of them in their thirties.

The 'permissive' '70s.

David, almost, his first question...

'And, how is Jim?'

Sophie, lying, saying, 'Oh, he's fine, fine.'

Surprised at how relieved she was that she had chosen this morning to wear the Monsoon dress, low neck, button front, taking advantage of the Indian summer, her hair, cut and high-lights – Toni and Guy – only two days before... aware, shocking herself, that she could fall into David's arms, again, just as easily as she had back then: Jim away with the band on endless tour, Aurelie started secondary school, Holland Park Comprehensive, Sophie with the novelty of time on her hands, wanting to take the next step, move out of Jim's shadow – his friends, his books, his records – make a life of her own, a career, even getting as far as to send off for and studying the Open University prospectus... Jim's illness putting paid to all that.

Putting paid to Sophie and David, too.

David saying, 'Still doing the music, is he?'

What they all said... people with humdrum occupations, who thought playing music was something you 'grew out of', no *real*

39

way to earn a living. Sophie remembering even her mother, Dorothy, a bohemian in her day, had read everything there was to read by and about the Bloomsbury Set – pilgrimage from Bath to Charleston House, West Sussex, a regular yearly event – Sophie teasing her, telling her Holly Johnson, Frankie Goes to Hollywood, was a fan of the Bloomsbury Set, private collection of paintings, Duncan Grant and Vanessa Bell: Sophie having to explain to her mother what 'fag hag' meant... even, Dorothy, saying, 'Yes, dear, that's all very well' – about Jim – 'but, when is he going to settle down, find himself a proper job?'

Still doing the music?

The only time any of them were ever impressed, when Jim appeared on the television – that, not very often – *Ready Steady Go, Top of the Pops, Old Grey Whistle Test*. For hours, afterwards, the phone ringing, 'Saw your Jim on that programme.'

Her friends.

Quite boring, really.

Saying to David, 'Of course. And yourself? I keep expecting to see your name in the papers, something high up in the civil service, you know, like Nigel Hawthorne in *Yes Minister*.'

Knowing she should be asking after Janet... the two children, what were their names? Horrified, realising they would be grown up, now, children of their own, most likely, David a grandparent.

David saying, 'I took early retirement.'

Sophie saying, 'Oh.'

What else could she say?

Are we really that old?

Hardly.

David saying, 'Funny, isn't it, careers master at school, all those jobs they assured you would be a cosy sinecure for life... banking, insurance, the civil service.'

A young boy on a mountain bike, buzz cut, camouflage pants, Nike Airs – Sophie thinking, Must have cost his mother a fortune – weaving along the crowded pavement at speed. David, 'Tut-tutting.' Sophie remembering just what an old fart David could be... that one weekend they had managed to get away together – Jim in the USA, supposed to be the band's break-through tour,

Aurelie in Bath with Sophie's parents, David, according to what he had told Janet, on a weekend Management Incentive Seminar in Birmingham – Wildecombe Manor Park, Dorset, candle-lit dinner for two, open fire, logs burning in the restaurant area, Verve Cliquot in an ice bucket delivered to their room... David unpacking his pyjamas, laying them out on the bed, asking Sophie which side would she prefer to sleep, concerned that they both had the same colour tooth brush – yellow – David saying, 'Wouldn't want to mix them up.' Sophie, unsure of her *own* role, naked beside the bed, saying, 'Oh, David!' Aware, then, of the attraction. David's absolute normalcy...

Compared to Jim.

David, now, saying, 'Look... standing here, why don't we have a coffee, or something?' Checking his watch, 'A drink, even, if it's not too early for you.'

Then: 'Campari and soda. Still your favourite tipple?'

Sophie, laughing, 'Oh, God! How '60s.'

'Seventies... '60s was rum and black.'

'That time I cooked for you—'

'Eggs Florentine.'

'You remember.'

'You can't get more '70s than eggs Florentine.'

'Proved you had earthenware dishes.'

Both of them laughing.

David saying, 'Well?'

Sophie, 'Well, what?'

7

Winston framed in the doorway – fuck were they doing in the master bedroom? – waiting for Robert, the daughter, one or both of them to notice his presence. The daughter, on her back, clutching Robert's hair between her fingers, pulling hard, legs wide apart, toes pointing at the ceiling, dark crimson nail polish, fingers and toes, Morticia, Anjelica Huston in *the Addam's Family*, only, much younger. Winston thinking, This woman is too pale, too small, too delicate to survive this kind of shagging. Robert's arse riding high in the air, then falling, his rhythm

41

metronome solid, the daughter gasping every time he began his descent, dove into her body.

Winston, unable to help noticing Robert's size.

Vlad the Impaler.

Fucking stroll on!

Wishing he had left it to Bobby-Boy, decided not to fuck him over – two grand for a walk-in? – give Robert time to get stuck in with the daughter, waltz in, lift the guitar.

Mother out.

Daughter occupied.

Piece of piss.

The daughter seeing Winston over Robert's shoulder.

Heavy duty security chain hanging from Winston's neck, cut-off denim jacket, bulging pectorals, tattooed biceps, saying, 'Who the fuck are you?'

Robert, looking round, answering her question, saying, 'Winston!'

The daughter saying, 'You two know each other?'

Pushing Robert away.

Then, saying: 'Threesomes, only by appointment. Sorry to disappoint.'

Not scared.

Winston realising she was on something.

The daughter, one step ahead of Winston, saying, 'Valium. My mother keeps a life-time's supply.'

Robert saying, 'Winston, this is Aurelie.'

Winston saying, 'You must have heard all the jokes by now.'

Aurelie saying, 'What do you want, Winston?'

Winston, surprising Aurelie, saying, 'Your old man's guitar.'

'My old man's guitar?'

'That's what I said.'

Aurelie, sitting up in the bed, not bothering to cover herself, thinking about it, saying, 'How come you knew about Jim's guitar?'

'Fender Telecaster... back of the wardrobe. You stuck to your own bedroom, would never have known I was here.'

Thinking of Bobby-Boy's story.

The weatherman.

Smiling.

Whole of fucking Chiswick into afternoon delights.

Saying, 'Lover-boy, here, he told me.'

Robert saying, 'Correction. I told Bobby-Boy. He was the one paid me.'

Aurelie saying, '*Paid* you! Am I hearing right?'

'I was going to tell you.'

Winston saying, 'That's what Bobby-Boy had figured. Not a smart move, Robert.'

Aurelie saying to Robert: 'Get the fuck out of my bed.'

Robert, on his feet,covering himself with his hands. Aurelie, then, to Winston: 'What would you give me for it?'

'What?'

'The guitar.'

'You'd sell it?'

'Why not?'

Winston saying, 'A hundred.'

'That much?'

'That much.'

'You know how old it is?'

'I know how old it is.'

Aurelie saying, 'Done.'

Robert, dressed now, hooded top, black mole-skin jeans, Puma trainers, saying, 'Aurelie—'

Winston saying, 'Not one word.'

'What about Bobby-Boy?'

'Big boy business.'

'I—'

'You still here?'

Robert opening his mouth to say it.

Winston saying, 'Don't say it.'

Robert thinking it, instead.

Heard all the stories.

What the fuck?

Bastard!

Winston saying, 'Don't even think it.'

43

Robert thinking, Fuck do you know, Mr Big-shot Winston-fucking-Capaldi?

Winston's fist landing in the centre of Robert's face.

Aurelie saying, 'You didn't need to do that.'

Then: 'Is it true what they say?'

'About what?'

'About steroids… that they shrink your nuts.'

chapter three

'See with your eyes!'

1

Sophie and David in the Barley Mow, Barley Mow Passage,
Sophie feeling safer meeting David at lunchtime rather than in the
evening. The pub decor: plaster and red brick distressed walls,
mismatched furniture, armchairs and settees, low wooden tables,
Sophie and David at a window seat overlooking Barley Mow
Passage, the design group complex across the way, a constant
procession of motor-cycle couriers entering and leaving the building, their stream-lined Japanese motor-cycles parked in the
Passage, radios squawking a cacophony of messages... David
drinking Guinness – 'We pick the one pub in Chiswick that does-
n't serve a decent pint of Fuller's,' – and a large scotch, Bells.
Sophie with a gin and tonic, David saying to the New Zealand
barman, 'Make that a large one, too,' not bothering to check first
with Sophie.

At the table, Sophie saying, 'You know, middle-age quite suits
you.'

David: 'Funny, isn't it, how we all have this built-in safety
device? Manage to convince ourselves we are better looking as we
get older... more distinguished.'

'You're not a woman.'

'And you've never suffered the humiliation of being invisible
to a woman.'

Then: '"Age cannot wither her…" '

'"Nor custom stale her infinite variety." '

Both of them laughing.

David saying, 'And you're not Cleopatra.'

Then: 'Nevertheless, I'm impressed.'

Sophie thinking, How patronising.

Sipping her gin and tonic.

Noticing David had finished his scotch.

Started on the Guinness.

Sophie saying, 'Don't be… we did it for A-Level.'

David saying, 'I'm divorced from Janet.'

Sophie: 'Jim is dead.'

David, silent a moment, then saying, 'I need another scotch… you?'

Motioning to Sophie's gin and tonic.

'I'm fine.'

David at the bar, Sophie remembering what Jim – no stranger to booze – had said about alcoholics. 'An alcoholic is someone always talking about how much they didn't drink.' And, that time, coming back from the neurology clinic at Charing Cross Hospital, laughing, the disease in its early stages, Jim filling out the registrar's questionnaire – previous ailments, history of diabetes? Epilepsy? Allergy to penicillin? Smoker or non-smoker? Daily average consumption of alcohol? – the doctor saying – Jim telling Sophie – 'An alcoholic is anybody who drinks more than a doctor.'

Wondering if David had a problem.

Fine pair, the two of them would make… David with his Bells whisky, Sophie, four ten-mil tabs of diazepam…

On a good day.

David back at the table.

Saying, 'Christ, Sophie, I'm so sorry.'

Then: 'How?'

And: 'When?'

Sophie saying, 'Actually, I don't want to talk about it.'

The same words she had spoken to Jim – the very same words – when he had brought up the subject of the funeral arrangements. Jim saying, 'No prayers, no hymns, right? I know the big temptation will be to just go along with it all, but, don't... otherwise, I'll come back and haunt you.' Handing Sophie a cassette tape, saying, 'I want this played at the end.' Everybody assuming it would be Otis Redding, 'Dock of the Bay', 'Mustang Sally', Wilson Picket, 'When a Man Loves a Woman', Percy Sledge, *anything* by Aretha Franklin... Jim a big soul fan, Steve Cropper his all-time favourite guitar player. The song on the cassette tape, 'Wish Me Luck As You Wave Me Goodbye'.

Gracie Fields.

The whole congregation laughing.

Couldn't help themselves.

Oh Jim! You fool.

Wishing he had kept his promise.

Come back to haunt her.

David saying, 'And, are you all right, I mean... money-wise?'

Sophie saying, 'I have the money from the sale of the house in Bath. Royalties from Jim's songs, not much, but, enough.'

Then: 'David, I don't feel comfortable with this.'

David saying, 'How do you mean?'

'You and me... it's different, now. Without Jim, without Janet, there is no safety net, no barrier to retreat behind.'

'You want to retreat?'

Sophie remembering, for months after the funeral, the phone never ringing, Sophie's friends embarrassed, not knowing what to say, happy enough on the subject of builders, mortgages, holidays, the kid's schooling... hopeless on death.

Sophie feeling that way now.

Stilted.

Saying, 'I don't want us becoming an item.'

David saying, 'For heaven's sake, Sophie, aren't we getting a little ahead of ourselves? It's not as if I've proposed marriage.'

Then: 'You know what they say, "A second marriage is the triumph of hope over experience." '

Sophie thinking, Is that such a bad thing?

Saying: 'That's exactly my point. I was never divorced. I was perfectly happy in my first marriage... Jim died, that's all.'

47

David, his scotch finished, looking towards the bar, saying, 'Is that why you ended it – us – Jim's illness?'

Sophie saying, 'It was none of your business.'

'You might have told me.'

'What would have been the point?'

'It might have helped.'

Sophie saying, 'David, what do you want from me?'

2

Charlie Paul pissed off with Bobby-Boy.

This time, really pissed off.

Sat in the Volkswagen Polo, C-reg, olive green – Bobby-Boy always saying, 'When you going to get yourself a decent motor?' Charlie saying, 'When I can afford one, Bobby-Boy' – eight doors up from where Bobby-Boy and Toyah lived, top two floors, four storey late-Victorian double frontage, Ravenscourt Road, rear of the house looking out over Ravenscourt Park. Bobby-Boy saying to Charlie, Charlie helping him and Toyah with the move, two years ago, already, 'Neighbours get nosy, I'll tell them I'm in security… lack of it, more like, am I right, Charlie?' Ever the joker. Charlie thinking, Bobby-Boy, you are one jammy bastard. Wondering, What was he doing here? Knowing he was in deep shit, Bobby-Boy ever had the least idea the way he felt about Toyah; Charlie supposed to be in Salford Avenue, taking care of business, checking out the daughter, Aurelie. Bobby-Boy saying, 'She has to have one regular habit in her life, otherwise it's not fucking natural. Take Toyah – for fuck's sake, *please* take Toyah – aerobics, aromatherapy, Spanish dance classes, now, she's talking about a fucking tattoo… always coming up with some new way to spend my money.' Charlie thinking: *Toyah! Toyah! Toyah!* How could she put up with this? How come women always went for the bastards? Did they *enjoy* being treated like shit? This, after last night, Bobby-Boy's Beamer, Bobby-Boy giving Charlie a lift home from Club 67, mobile on the dash going off – Charlie didn't see it in the dark – frightened the life out of him… not expecting to hear a telephone. Bobby-Boy saying, 'Well, answer it, for fuck's sake.' Charlie picking the mobile up off the dash, still ringing,

48

saying to Bobby-Boy, 'What do I do?' Bobby-Boy grabbing the phone, saying, 'Join the modern world, why don't you?'

Pressing OK.

Charlie hearing Toyah's voice.

Bobby-Boy saying, 'The fuck is it to you?'

Then: 'I need a talking clock, I'll let you know.'

Pressing something on the phone.

Throwing it back on the dash.

Saying, 'Fucking tart.'

Toyah! Toyah! Toyah!

Charlie thinking, Is this how it happens?

How you become a stalker?

Picturing himself locking the car, walking up to the house, climbing the stairs to the porch, stone lion on either side, guarding the entrance… ringing the bell. Toyah coming down the hall, opening the front door, wearing what? Towelling dressing gown? Towelling dressing gown sounded good… belted loosely at the waist. Toyah saying, 'What kept you, Charlie?'

Taking his hand.

Leading him inside.

Closing the door.

It not mattering that Charlie had never made love to a woman before in his life – the only woman he had ever loved before Toyah, his mother, God rest her soul, been gone ten years, now, when Charlie was thirty – Toyah undressing him slowly, shrugging off the dressing gown, coming to Charlie, gently initiating him into the art of love-making, desire, arousal, satiation… the two of them eventually falling asleep in each other's arms.

Bobby-Boy?

He could go fuck himself.

Seeing a minicab draw up in the road outside where Bobby-Boy and Toyah lived, the driver sitting there sounding his horn, Charlie thinking, 'Lazy fucker.'

Winston Capaldi coming down the steps.

Getting into the cab.

3

Winston taking the minicab – Peugeot 306 Saloon, Winston's favourite ride – straight from Toyah to Aurelie, not sure how much more of this he could take, how much he *wanted* to take. Toyah: 'You know ways of hurting me... without it showing?' Winston thinking, What is the problem? Bobby-Boy finds out, he can beat the shit out of you, ought to keep you happy, saying, 'Without showing? You must be confusing me with the Filth.' Remembering the scene in an American film, watched it on video, gangster punishing a woman in his hotel room, thought she had been skimming off the top, bag of oranges – no bruises – trying to imagine himself, Toyah, bag of oranges, saying to Toyah, 'This is getting too heavy.' Toyah saying, 'Don't advertise what you can't deliver.' Little finger through the gold ring in his nipple, pulling. Winston's eyes watering... her mouth closing around his prick – tongue teasing *that* ring – the pressure of her teeth, an unspoken threat. Winston saying, an attempt to lighten things up, 'You're thinking short-term, Toyah.' Reminded of the story – no idea if it was true – how a Thai woman would cut off her man's prick, no hesitation, she found out he had been with another woman... Thai men, as a precaution, always keeping a bowl of ice underneath the bed, put the severed prick in, keep it fresh on the way to the nearest hospital. Toyah, releasing him a moment, saying, 'Who said anything about long-term?' Winston saying, 'Selfish bitch.'

Coming in her mouth.

And, now, Aurelie.

Saying, over the phone, 'You know what? I think my mother has got herself a boyfriend.'

Winston saying, 'That so strange?'

Then: 'Your mother is a good-looking woman.'

'Like mother, like daughter?'

Winston saying, 'I'm using you to get to her.'

'Bastard.'

Winston saying, 'Only the once, I'll tell you this... don't ever call me that again.'

'Touchy!'

'Believe it.'

Aurelie saying, 'Dear me, our very first row.'

Now, in the minicab, short trip, Hammersmith to Grove Park, Winston not seen this driver before, giving Winston the run-around – he would learn – passing the turn-off to Chiswick Town Hall, Sutton Court Road, instead, going as far as Kew Bridge before turning off to the left, the driver deciding the only reason Winston hired cabs, he was starved of conversation, saying to Winston, 'Jason, right... my name? According to insurance company statistics, that makes me a high risk driver – just the name.' And: 'Listen, it gets worse. I'm born in March... Pisces.' Catching Winston's eye in the rear-view mirror.. 'Did you know that star sign has the highest claims record for smashed wind-screens?'

Winston saying nothing.

The driver saying, 'I kid you not.'

Then: 'Salesmen, nightclub owners, models, demolition men, dispatch riders and mini-cab drivers... all high premium occupations. My own time, I drive a Corsa SXi, Vauxhall. What do you think my insurance costs me every year?'

Winston still saying nothing.

The driver saying, 'Hazard a guess.'

Winston saying, 'Did you ever have an accident?'

'That's what's so unfair.'

Winston saying, 'Good fortune may be about to desert you.'

Pulling up in Salford Avenue.

Winston getting out of the cab, coming round to the driver's side, the driver saying, 'That will be five-fifty.'

Winston handing him three pounds, saying, 'That includes the tip... buy yourself an *A to Z*.'

4

Dennis Lightfoot, aka Dennis the Dice, aka Dicey, aka The Diceman – all these names attributed to Dennis on account of his first entrepreneurial killing, back in the '70s, shipment of furry dice, originally earmarked for Halford's of Ealing, electric pink, blue, yellow. Dennis saying, so the story went, 'These dice will consign the nodding dog forever to the dustbin of history,' – saying, now, to Bobby-Boy and Charlie Paul, 'It's amazing what you can do in one day compared to what you don't do most days.'

Propping up the bar, Club 67, none of the evening regulars in yet, Dennis wearing his usual trench-coat, gabardine, collar turned up, thought he was Humphrey Bogart... The Diceman so geriatric he still called a telephone 'the blower'.

Bobby-Boy thinking, Price you pay.

Next, the old sod would be banging on about car boot sales and what a genius it was came up with that one.

Pound shops.

Another favourite subject.

Dennis saying, expecting a laugh, 'Except in Lewisham... they still got 60p shops in Lewisham.'

Then: Nationwide distribution.

Old Bill, not a clue...

Heard it all before.

Bobby-Boy saying, 'Can't argue with that, Dennis.'

Charlie Paul still seeing Winston coming down the steps.

Getting in the cab.

Cat got the cream.

Saying, 'Don't talk to me about today... I would just as soon forget it.'

Dennis, not listening, saying, 'Cheer up, Charlie, it may never happen.'

Charlie Paul saying, 'It already did.'

Beryl behind the bar serving drinks, her regular barman not due in till nine o'clock... Bobby-Boy in the chair, ordered three large scotches; with ice, for himself, coke and ice for Charlie, The Diceman, straight up, Dennis making a big show of adding three drops of water from the jug on the bar top, saying, 'I do hope this is plain tap water, none of your foreign muck?' Bobby-Boy saying to Beryl, 'You know, it's customary, nowadays, few nibbles on the bar for the customers?'

Beryl Ulanowski.

Seen it all.

Done it all...

Bought the club in '87, when it was called the Three Gs, a members only drinking club, the then owner feeling the pinch due to the new 'all day drinking' licensing laws, gave Beryl a good price. Beryl, with big hair, flame red, changing the name to Red Sonja's, coming in every night dressed in a low-cut leather bodice, leather mini-skirt, thigh-length leather boots with six inch heels, the club membership increasing by a hundred and fifty per cent over six months – all strictly, look don't touch. On her fiftieth birthday, deciding her alter-ego, Red Sonja, was undignified for a woman of her years, Beryl revamped the club, hired in a '60s specialist DJ four nights a week, hung psychedelic posters on the walls, broken electric guitars from the ceiling – she swore they had all been smashed by Pete Townsend – renamed the club, Club 67, invited Jenny Fabian, '60s author of *Groupie*, as her special guest on the opening night. Her only mistake had been the inflatable furniture...

Didn't last five minutes.

Well, maybe a week.

Beryl saying, now, 'This a celebration?'

Then: 'Not every day we see Bobby-Boy pushing the boat out.'

The Diceman, raising his glass, saying, 'Clarice Cliff.'

Adding: 'Sonja.'

Knowing Beryl hated it – what could she do? – Dennis still missing the low-cut leather bodice... especially the thigh boots.

Then: 'Globe teapot, biscuit jar, ginger jar, empire teacup and saucer, candlestick, all as featured in the original Newport Pottery sales leaflet, 1928, Original Bizarre.'

Beryl saying, 'Original Bizarre?'

Bobby-Boy saying, 'Don't say it, Beryl.'

Seen it coming.

Knowing how touchy The Diceman could be.

On the surface, a bundle of laughs, but you wouldn't want to get on the wrong side of The Diceman... personal invite to Ronnie's funeral, more lock-ups under more names than the Queen Mother had body servants, never felt once, despite – Dennis's words – a lifetime in the 'redistribution industry'. Popular parlance had it that when The Diceman finally did retire, even Old Bill would chip in for his gold watch.

The Diceman.

53

Bobby-Boy's 'wholesaler'.

Principle fence.

Bobby-Boy saying, 'Shout it from the roof-tops, why don't you?'

The Clarice Cliff Collection, a Bobby-Boy score. Georgian Terrace, off the river, end of Black Lion Lane. Bobby-Boy breaking one of his own golden rules – never shit on your own doorstep – but thinking, What the fuck! AP Herbert used to live in one of them… Bobby-Boy, since he was a kid, always wanting to know what the houses looked like from the inside, how the other half lived. Told people about AP Herbert, they would say, 'The fuck is AP Herbert?'

Bobby-Boy deciding…

You had to be local.

Beryl saying, 'Clarice Cliff?'

Bobby-Boy giving Dennis the look.

Dennis, ignoring Bobby-Boy, saying, 'A rags to riches story, Sonja, straight out of Mills and Boon. Poor factory girl has twenty year affair with factory owner on her path to fame, fortune, and artistic recognition. Finally marries the factory owner after the death of his crippled wife.'

Beryl saying, 'I'm none the wiser.'

Then, to Bobby-Boy and Charlie: 'You know what he's on about?'

Charlie saying, 'You're not supposed to use the word "crippled" any more.'

Dennis saying, 'Oh, fuck off, Charlie!'

Raising his glass, again.

Saying, 'To our Belgian friends.'

Bobby-Boy saying, 'You made the deal?'

'Why we're here, Bobby-Boy.'

Charlie saying to Bobby-Boy, 'This mean we're flush?'

Bobby-Boy saying, 'We?'

Clocking Charlie Paul's expression.

Saying: 'Oh, fuck off, Charlie!'

Aurelie saying, about Winston and Aurelie doing it in her bedroom, 'It doesn't feel right. I spent my childhood in this room. I believed in Father Christmas in this room. Decided to commit suicide in this room when I heard that Simon Le Bon was getting married.'

'Simon Le Bon?'

'Duran Duran.'

'I know that.'

Winston thinking, Jesus!

Saying, 'Who else did you like?'

'You'll hate me for it.'

'Go on.'

Aurelie saying, 'Human League, Spandau Ballet, Ultravox.'

Winston, this time, saying it: 'Jesus!'

Aurelie saying, 'Well, I was young.'

'Not that young.'

'Fourteen.'

Winston in remand home, Haversham, at fourteen.

Not about to tell Aurelie.

Saying, 'Fourteen is no excuse.'

'I was a late developer.'

Aurelie remembering her father, Jim, bursting into the room – this very room – shouting to be heard, saying, 'Turn that racket down!' 'Save a Prayer', Duran Duran... or was it 'Hungry Like a Wolf'?

Jim horrified.

Saying, 'Was that me?'

Then: 'Did I really just say that?'

Another time, Jim saying, 'Why don't you listen to something decent, at least? Pick a band who can play musical instruments.'

And, when Marcus started coming round, Jim a musician, Marcus thinking he would want to talk about turn-tables, tape decks, CDs, available for the first time in the shops, Jim saying, 'The "come round and listen to my speakers" syndrome... greatest threat to real music the world has ever known.'

Aurelie not understanding what her father meant.

Still didn't.

Knowing he was frustrated.

Felt on the scrap-heap.

Not much older than Aurelie now...

Standing in the doorway.

Winston behind her.

Pressing close.

Aurelie thinking, It was this room, too, that I came back to after Jim died. Telling Marcus I needed space... time to think. Sat on the edge of the bed and wondered why the tears would not come.

Feeling guilty.

Feckless.

Not worthy as a daughter.

Winston's hands circling her breasts.

Aurelie saying, 'Not much to write home about.'

Winston saying, 'Seek and ye shall find.'

Aurelie saying, 'Would you mind?'

'Mind what?'

'If we didn't.'

Winston stroking Aurelie's stomach.

Finger teasing her navel.

Saying, 'Did you ever consider a stud?'

Then: 'You are taking the piss, aren't you?'

6

Robert, a large square of white gauze bandage taped across his nose covering the centre of his face entirely, eyes peering out from the top two corners of the bandage, the tape, that flimsy hospital see-through stuff, the ends torn, not even cut neatly with a pair of scissors. Bobby-Boy thinking, You would have thought, in hospital, they would have had a decent pair of scissors.

Robert's voice, sounding like somebody was attempting to smother him with a pillow – not such a bad idea – saying, 'This is your fault, Bobby-Boy.'

Bobby-Boy saying, 'Christ! Your face looks a mess. Is that as bad as it looks?'

Cordova's, Chiswick High Road.

Bobby-Boy, *café latte*.

Robert, Diet Coke, with a straw.

Bobby-Boy listening to the conversation at the next table, two women, one doing all the talking, the woman saying, 'So, the girl in the bank said, "And did you have a nice holiday?" And I said, "Why are you all wearing red T-shirts?" She said: "It's a mortgage promotion... do you have a mortgage?" "Yes," I said, and she said, "Who with?" so, I told her, "Britannia." "Would you like to change to us?" she said, and I said, "Why, because you're wearing red T-shirts?" '

The two women laughing.

Bobby-Boy thinking, Hilarious.

Saying, to Robert, 'You need that straw?'

Robert saying, 'It helps, I don't move my face around too much.'

Bobby-Boy saying, 'It was a dumb move, Robert. You don't fuck with the customers.'

Then: 'My customers.'

'Customers?'

'Modern focus group terminology, Robert. You were in hospital having that nose set, you were a customer, not a patient.'

'Fuck all difference it made, time I had to wait.'

'That's the whole point.'

'How do you mean?'

'You got a pile of shit, you call it faecal discharge.'

'What discharge?'

'Forget it – it's still a pile of shit.'

'Isn't that what I was just saying?'

'Welcome to the modern world, Robert.'

The woman at the next table, still the same woman, saying, now, 'Sometimes, you get so used to charity shop prices, you get surprised how cheap things are new.' The two women with white wine spritzers, eating *croque monsieurs*, cutting every piece with a knife, fussy eaters, both of them. The woman saying, 'Amazing just how uncharitable women who work in charity shops can be.' The other woman saying, 'Bit sweeter on the whiskers front.'

Bobby-Boy thinking, Fuck is she talking about?

Whiskers front?

The woman saying, 'You know, the really old dears.'

As if she knew Bobby-Boy was listening.

Needed a translation.

'She was offering it on a plate, Bobby-Boy.'

'Oh really? And that makes it all right?'

'There was no reason to set Winston on me – fucking animal.'

'You don't lip Winston.'

'I never said a word.'

'Way I heard it, you were giving it some.'

'I never said a fucking word!'

Bobby-Boy watching the two women, both mid-thirties, dressed down, one of them, grey cowl-neck jumper, the other – the one doing most of the talking – black cardigan over a grey top, everything monochrome, except, both of them with short blonde hair, like that radio DJ, TV presenter – Zöe Ball? – pushed back off the forehead... the hair, the clothes, expensive, designed to look thrown together. Bobby-Boy thinking, What *was* the fucking point? You had the money, you let people know... flaunted it. Only, in his case that was not an option. Old Bill... The Inland Revenue. It didn't bear thinking about. Wondering if either of the women had a tattoo on *her* arse... last night, Bobby-Boy, well out of it by the time he made it upstairs to bed, Toyah undressing, making a big thing of it, hand stroking her backside, saying, 'Well, what do you think?'

On Toyah's arse, left buttock, cross between an owl and a parrot – Bobby-Boy deciding the tattoo artist *must* be taking the piss, never seen a stranger looking bird – stubby wings, talons spread... the bird and the feathers outlined in blue, filled in green, except for the eyes. The eyes were yellow. Bobby-Boy saying, 'The fuck is that?'

Toyah saying, 'A kakapo.'

'You've got to be kidding?'

'Flightless parrot.'

Then: 'I wanted something different.'

'Well, congratulations.'

'Comes from New Zealand. I saw it on one of those natural

58

history programmes... with David Attenborough. The male of the species plods all the way up a mountain, puffs himself up like a bullfrog, sends out this mating call, hoping to attract a female. There are only about seventy kakapos left in the world.'

Bobby-Boy saying, 'Can you fucking wonder.'

Thinking, Tattoos?

Kakapoos?

What the fuck is going on?

Toyah saying, 'Do anything for you?'

Bobby-Boy saying, 'What? A flightless fucking parrot?'

'Pedestrian.'

'Say, again?'

'What they call a flightless bird... "pedestrian".'

Then: 'It said so in the programme.'

Then: 'You didn't answer my question.'

'Not a thing.'

'Bobby-Boy, you are lying.'

First time in how long?

The two of them at it like a pair of rabbits, Bobby-Boy making a joke, saying, 'Fat chance... we were a pair of kakapo.' Toyah saying, 'I'm not made of porcelain, Bobby-Boy. I'm not going to break.' Bobby-Boy wondering, again, What the fuck is going on?

Saying, now, to Robert, 'Could have been worse.'

'How's that?'

'I've known Winston a long time. He's one crazy fucker.'

'Very nice... a psychopath for a friend.'

The two women arguing over which of them was going to pay the bill, both waving Switch cards, Bobby-Boy saying to Robert, 'Hardly a friend.'

The girl pushing in through the swing doors.

Sporty top, red, blue and white, zip neck.

Track bottoms, blue with white piping.

White trainers.

Bobby-Boy, not knowing who she was till she took off the Nike wraparound sunglasses, placing her, finally, thinking, Oh, shit!

Yvonne.

The weatherman.

Robert saying, 'Too fucking right.'

'What?'

'He tell you he bought the guitar?'

Yvonne, seeing Bobby-Boy, coming over to where Bobby-Boy and Robert were sitting, hovering at the table, easing the weight of her shoulder bag, not certain what she was starting, saying to Bobby-Boy, 'I know you?'

Bobby-Boy, half listening to Robert, saying, 'You sure you want to know?'

Yvonne rolling her eyes.

Bobby-Boy saying, 'Didn't recognise you... not with your pants on.'

'Excuse me!'

Bobby-Boy, saying to Robert, 'Bought the guitar?'

Yvonne saying, 'Gary's place!'

'Do me a favour.'

'As in, "Mum's the word"?'

'No, as in, "You must be fucking joking".'

Yvonne considering.

Then, leaning forward, smiling, whispering in Bobby-Boy's ear, more breath than was necessary, saying, 'I never met a bona fide burglar before.'

'We're nothing special.'

The two women leaving, 20p on the table for the waitress, the talkative one saying, 'My Philip was furious... I told him, "Five minutes, I was gone. No more than that." Eighty pounds *and* I had to wait two hours.'

On the pavement, now.

The other woman nodding sympathetically.

Bobby-Boy thinking, I'm in the wrong fucking game.

Robert saying, 'The Telecaster... a hundred quid.'

Bobby-Boy saying, 'Winston *bought* the Telecaster?'

Then: 'A hundred quid!'

'From the daughter.'

'Bastard!'

Yvonne, pulling out a seat, sitting down, parking her shoulder bag on the floor at her feet, saying to Robert, 'What happened to your face?'

Robert saying, 'I thought what he just said.'

Yvonne saying, 'You guys are crazy.'

Bobby-Boy saying, 'Tell me about it.'

chapter four

'Way to go!'

1

Jim on death.

The great hereafter.

Sophie had kept the studio cassette.

Listening to it, now.

God knows why.

GLR – Greater London Radio – programme, broadcast three-thirty, Tuesday afternoon, April 2nd, 1995. Jim excited that he had been invited on the show, talk programme, 'The Way We Were', Barbra Streisand song as the theme music... Sophie speaking to the production office, checking ease of drop-off in Marylebone High Street, wheel-chair access, toilet facilities, letting the production team know this would not be easy.

Karen Mitchell, the show's presenter, contacted specifically, agreeing to waive the studio NO SMOKING policy – just this once. Jim feeling honoured... very special. Sophie thinking, Oh, Jim! You poor bastard. You *deserved* to feel very special.

His voice, on tape, cracked.

Hesitant.

Each inhalation – oxygen or nicotine – a goal achieved.

A Pyrrhic victory.

Karen Mitchell asking about the disease.

The multiple sclerosis.

Jim saying, 'When you are a kid death means nothing. It only ever happens to other people. Then, you hit the Big Three, see the far end of the line, you think, Oh, my God! This is too horrifying... the realisation that it not only might, but, most definitely *will* happen to you. Death... finito... the big void. It's not, so much, you are worried *how* it is going to happen, more, that it is entirely beyond your comprehension – that endless infinity – all that time, *forever*, when you will not be there. How could the world possibly exist without you?'

The performer kicking in, Jim, realising he needed to lighten up, saying, 'Imagine... a time when the worst thing about being dead is that you will never get to hear the new Who LP. Or, never know if the next Georgie Fame single was even better than "Yeah! Yeah!"'

Karen Mitchell saying, 'It's interesting that you should still use that expression.'

Jim, accepting the feed, saying, 'What expression?'

'LP... Long Player.'

'For the benefit of our younger listeners. Yes, well, we never used to wear crash helmets in those days, either.'

'I don't follow?'

'What I'm saying is... it was all a very long time ago.'

Karen Mitchell leading Jim through the history of The Crunch, the early west London club scene, the tours, the two albums, *Oceans Away* and *Afterthought*, the falling out with Decca Records. Jim laughing, saying, about the title of the second and last album, 'Too bloody right! *Afterthought*, indeed.' The 'bloody' sounding strange, Jim not done this in a long time, uncertain if he could get away with 'fucking' on the radio. Karen playing 'Crystal Crusader', from the first album, then the Tom Jones cover, 'Maybe Tomorrow', Karen saying, 'Did you know there was a Billy Fury song called "Maybe Tomorrow"?' Jim saying, 'Who's Billy Fury?'

Then: 'Only joking.'

Karen asking, When did Jim realise there might be something wrong, that he might have a serious illness. Was he on stage, performing, playing his instrument...

Like Jacqueline du Pré?

Jim saying, 'No, I was slicing carrots.'

Then: 'Do you want to know what I really resent about my illness? That I can look into a goldfish bowl and think, That fucking goldfish is going to live longer than I am.'

Finally, saying it.

Fucking.

Live radio.

Karen Mitchell – Jim telling Sophie later – placing a finger in front of her lips, nodding her head, saying, 'This is Karen Mitchell, "The Way We Were", talking to Jim Grace of The Crunch – we'll be back after the news and traffic update. Stay with us, GLR, 94.9.' Then, to Jim, 'We are going to have to watch the expletives, Jim.'

Jim saying: 'I just wet myself.'

Sophie, now, hearing the phone ringing.

Knowing it would be David.

David saying, 'Give it a chance, Sophie... that's all I'm asking.'

Carefully enunciating every word.

Every syllable.

Did he expect Sophie not to realise he was drunk?

Sophie thinking, Why Jim?

Why not David?

2

Bobby-Boy saying, 'Those are, disgusting... even the smell.'

Thinking, The fuck am I doing here?

Yvonne saying, '*They* don't seem to mind.'

Meaning, the ducks.

Bobby-Boy and Yvonne, far side of the stone ornamental bridge, cricket pitch back there behind the trees, Yvonne throwing Fangs to the ducks, found the packet in her shoulder bag when she was looking for cigarettes... vinegar flavour, Christ knows how long they had been in the shoulder bag. Bobby-Boy thinking, Yvonne probably not even *born* last time I was in Chiswick Park, giving her a Marlboro, lighting it with a disposable, Yvonne saying, 'Smart lighter for a burglar,' Bobby-Boy saying, about the Fangs, 'Make your mouth stink.'

Yvonne saying, 'Why should you care?'

Then: 'When I was a kid, used to be a violinist, played in the trees, you could hear him from anywhere in the park... wasn't very good.'

Telling Bobby-Boy about the colony of parakeets.

Saying, 'Is that what you would call them... a colony?'

And: 'Listen, if you concentrate, you can hear them.'

Asking Bobby-Boy about his name...

Bobby-Boy no idea how he had first come by the name, the 'Boy' tagged on – like *bach*, in Welsh, meaning 'love' – Bobby-Boy liking to believe the 'Boy' was a term of endearment. His mother, when she was alive, had called him Robert. His father, now in an NHS trust home in Ruislip – Alzheimer's – had called him Bob. What he called Bobby-Boy, now, was anybody's guess. Last time Bobby-Boy had visited him, his father had pointed out the window – landscaped gardens, an avenue of oak – saying, 'My son, he did all that.' Bobby-Boy saying, 'All what, Dad?' Bobby-Boy's dad saying, 'Those trees... he planted them.' Then: 'Every one of them.' Another time, before the doctors and the social workers decided he would be better off in – their term – a super-vised environment, Bobby-Boy's father had rung Bobby-Boy by mistake on his mobile, thought he had dialled the Midland Bank, saying, when he heard Bobby-Boy's voice, 'That you, Bob?' Then: 'What are you doing in the bank?'

When did 'eccentric' slide, unnoticed, into something entirely different? How was it measured? The consultant, at Ealing Hospital, telling Bobby-Boy, 'With Alzheimer's Disease we have a scale of one to thirty. Your father is between four and five.' Bobby-Boy saying, 'The wrong end of the scale?' The consultant saying, 'The wrong end of the scale.'

Bobby-Boy telling Yvonne about his father.

Not sure why.

Never spoke to *anybody* about his father.

Yvonne saying, 'What's it like?'

'What's what like?'

'Being a criminal?'

'Is that what this is all about?'

Yvonne, laughing, saying, 'Why, did you think I wanted your body?'

Coming level with the big house, Chiswick House, the other side of the water, ducks still following them, wake disturbing the reeds on the far bank, shaking loose a moorhen, the bird leaving its nest to investigate... Bobby-Boy remembering he used to come here with his *I Spy* book, *I Spy Birds*, ticking off the entries as he identified each bird – wouldn't have dreamed of cheating – his finest hour, not in Chiswick Park, but on Wimbledon Common, when he spotted a sparrowhawk; sending off the completed book to *I Spy*, waiting for his feather to arrive in the post. Saying, now, to Yvonne, 'That used to be the Duke of Norfolk's house. This was all his private estate. My grandad and his mates used to bunk in over the wall to play when they were kids.'

Then: 'It's a job of work... like any other.'

Telling Yvonne about his network of stringers. Glaziers, scaffolders, minicab drivers, postmen, dustmen, plumbers, sparkies, gardeners... saying, 'Your postman, for example, he delivers a copy of *Coin Collector's Monthly* on subscription, that is information worth having. Holiday dates, specific items of value – the dustman notices the packaging for a new i-Mac computer in the rubbish... bingo! – interior layouts, whether there are any pets – even a goldfish means a neighbour coming in to feed it.'

Telling Yvonne his golden rule, 'Never – ever – go in when you suspect there might be somebody in the house.'

Telling Yvonne about Yale High Security, the Mark IV Trifid, Micromark Observation Systems and Fortress Infrared Detectors, the Mul-T-Lock Euro half interactive cylinder, saying, 'Pin registration for duplicate keys, pick *and* drill resistant, but, is it kick-proof?'

Yvonne saying, 'Sounds technical.'

Bobby-Boy saying, 'It doesn't have to be. There are still people leave their front door key under a milk bottle.'

Telling Yvonne, 'Householders, they leave the hall light on all day. You think, well, thank you very much... now, I *know* there's no-one home.'

Telling Yvonne... the game he liked to play, in a crowded pub or restaurant, thinking, law of averages, seeing a woman at the bar – for example – imagining she was one of his past customers, that he knew all her secrets, had been through her bottom drawer, read her private letters.

Yvonne saying, 'Customers?'

Bobby-Boy saying, 'What I call them... the people I rob. It's almost as if I should be sending them a bottle of scotch, a card, at Christmas.'

Saying: 'I don't hold with those dirty bastards, big chip on their shoulder, leave their call-sign, crap all over the bed. That's disgusting... they *deserve* to be locked up.'

Telling Yvonne he didn't consider himself to be above the law... it was just that, nine times out of ten, he didn't see it as applying to himself.

Saying, 'Why am I telling you all this?'

Yvonne saying, 'You're weird... you know that?'

Then: 'You married?'

Bobby-Boy saying, 'I look married?'

'It doesn't bother me, either way.'

'I noticed that... with the weatherman.'

Yvonne singing...

Steve Harley tune.

'*You've seen it all.*'

Then: 'Why did we come here... Chiswick Park?'

'It's the last place on earth I'd expect to meet anybody I know.'

'Ashamed of me?'

'I'm twice your age.'

The ducks given up.

Gone back to the shelter of the bridge.

Yvonne saying, 'So? What are we doing?'

Then: 'All we are doing is talking.'

3

Charlie Paul caught up with Toyah outside Sing My Body Electric, health complex opposite L & M Motors, Chiswick High Road, Toyah about to go in, check out at reception what manual lymphatic drainage could do for her body, spotting Charlie coming up behind her along the pavement... Charlie, straight away, reminding her of the kakapo bird she had tattooed on her arse, something in the way he walked, shoulders swinging from side to side, Toyah saying, 'Charlie Paul. You following me?'

Charlie looking everywhere but at Toyah.

Toyah saying, 'Look, maybe you can help me, here. Lymphatic drainage... what do you think?'

Charlie, confusing lymphatic drainage with liposuction, saying, 'I don't see you having a weight problem, Toyah.'

'Well, you're a sweety for saying that, Charlie.'

Toyah looking gorgeous – feeling gorgeous – decided this year's black was black, dressed in a knee-length single breasted leather coat, from Episode, split leather mini skirt, black fishnets, kitten-heeled bar shoes, the shoes from Pied a Terre, set Bobby-Boy back ninety-nine quid – he didn't know that, yet – Toyah saying to Charlie, 'It's not about fat. It's to do with detoxification, decongestion, relaxation.'

Then: 'Did you know... your lymphatic system is responsible for the elimination of all the toxins in your body?'

Charlie Paul saying, 'It's not to do with hoovering fat off your stomach?'

'Charlie!'

Toyah remembering some of the things Bobby-Boy had said about Charlie Paul... how when his mother died – he was still caretaker at Hogarth School – Charlie had asked the school secretary if he could have passionate leave. How in Kalamari, Greek restaurant along the High Road, he had insisted on ordering *Torremolinos* as a starter. How Bobby-Boy had witnessed Charlie's moment of revelation, Freddy Mercury in the ground two years, Charlie saying, '*Queen!* As in "poofta"... as in "queer".' Covering himself, saying, 'It's the name of a band, right? You don't think about it too much... the name of a band.' Bobby-Boy, telling Toyah the story, laughing, saying, 'Fuck knows what he would make of the Pet Shop Boys.'

Toyah saying, 'What *about* the Pet Shop Boys?'

Bobby-Boy saying, 'Hamsters?'

'What about hamsters?'

Bobby-Boy saying, 'Forget it.'

Toyah, now, saying to Charlie, 'What *are* you doing here, Charlie?'

4

Winston seeing red.

Already, his day fucked up.

Eric Holtz, in London on other business, agreed to meet Winston, briefly, saying, over the telephone, 'Twenty minutes, this is all I have, OK?' And: 'Authentication is not a problem... I can arrange authentication.' And: 'Winston, you have to remember... for me this is small change. I do this as a favour, right?' Winston trying hard to remember the last time Eric Holtz did *anybody* a favour, waiting in the first floor lounge bar, looking down over the station concourse, Kings Cross, one-thirty through to three-thirty, two, three thousand profit on the guitar not small change to Winston, Eric Holtz his only conduit to the Japanese. Winston keeping all this in mind while he waited, knowing, by two-thirty, that Eric Holtz was not going to show... still waiting the extra hour.

Now, four-fifteen.

Chiswick Park Station.

District Line.

Somebody telling Winston, once, the building was of great architectural interest, saying, 'You remember the Firestone Building, on the Great West Road? Got knocked down by developers... Chiswick Park Station is the same period, thirties Art Deco.'

Winston not giving a flying fuck.

Then or now.

The man blocking his path, black, uniform blue, black and yellow striped band on his hat... big, looked like he would moonlight as a club bouncer, saying, 'Would you step over here a moment?'

His two companions, young, slim Indian man, white woman, talking to a girl carrying a musical instrument case, got off the same train as Winston.

Instrument probably a violin.

The girl close to tears.

Winston saying, 'I am stepping nowhere.'

Already offered the difference in fare, explaining how he had changed his mind, decided not to get off at Turnham Green, instead, stayed on the one extra stop to Chiswick Park, thought he would pick up a cab from there, go see Aurelie, in Grove Park, hope her good-looking mother was home – Aurelie, too precious by far, wouldn't *that* surprise her. Winston keeping this last part – Aurelie and her mother – to himself. The ticket inspector saying, 'You should have decided on your destination *before* commencing your journey.' And: 'You do not have a valid ticket for travel… you are, therefore, required to pay an excess charge of £10.'

Winston understanding the look.

Two big blokes…

This wasn't work.

It was personal.

Saying, 'Bollocks.'

Head-butting the ticket inspector.

The ticket inspector, reeling back, loosing his official cool, saying, 'Fuck's with you, man?'

Then: 'Bastard!'

Winston saying, 'Now, you really have done it.'

Wondering how much shit he could kick out of Mr Big, still be long gone before the police arrived.

5

Sophie remembering Jim taking the acoustic guitar he kept lying around the house, playing her the last song he ever wrote… after The Crunch had lost their recording contract, broken up. Jim saying, 'It's a ballad… picture Harry Nilson, Roy Orbison, even, just standing there in front of the microphone, eyes front, like a rock, strumming four to the bar…'

Singing…

'Love knows,

For every candle burning low,

There's a shadow that will grow,

70

Love knows,
Love knows,
For every star that lights the sky,
There's a flame will fade and die,
Love knows, love knows,
Oh love knows,
For every fire that burns below,
There's a tide will ebb and flow,
Love knows, oh love knows…'

Jim saying, still playing, 'Nice little modulation here, instrumental section, keep it simple… cello, maybe, playing the tune.'

Singing…

'Love knows,
For every day gives way to night,
There's a moon reflects the light
Love knows, love knows,
Oh love knows,
For every wind of change that blows,
There's an ember still that glows,
God knows –
Oh, God knows.'

Sophie, always embarrassed when Jim played her anything, never sure what to say, how to fill the ensuing silence. This time, quite certain. Saying, 'But, that's beautiful, Jim. Almost hymnal.'

Jim, tossing the guitar onto the sofa, saying, 'What the fuck. You could write "Moon River" nowadays and nobody would notice.'

Sophie saying, 'Bitterness doesn't suit you, Jim.'

6

The café in the Park.

Floral pattern oil-cloths covering the tables, on each table a jug with a plastic sunflower, in the centre of each sunflower a table number surrounded by yellow petals – used to be formica table-tops and council-green fold-up bandstand chairs… sat on them for five minutes, felt like you had been caned on the arse, six of the best.

Bobby-Boy remembering what that felt like...

The very last – ever – boy to be caned at his school.

Before the media witch-hunts began.

All teachers became closet perverts.

Fucking joke, that was.

Didn't they know anything?

Bobby-Boy and Yvonne, both with cups of tea.

Large... too weak.

Behind Yvonne, the counter the same, stretching the length of the back of the café, tea and coffee machines at the far end beside the till, chalk board with 'Today's Special': broccoli and Stilton soup, ciabatta roll and butter, various cakes in a glass cabinet, slices cut to order... triple chocolate and toffee, nut fudge, coffee, carrot and banana, wedges of flapjack for the wholefood health freaks. The frontage, too, unchanged. Floor to ceiling glass panelled, central door, overlooking grass and a hedgerow, horse chestnut trees, outside seating... crunch of gravel underfoot as people came and went.

Bobby-Boy remembering being here as a kid, Sunday afternoons, with his mum and dad, his mum saying, 'You don't eat that you'll get a good slap,' his father saying, 'Money doesn't grow on trees, son.'

Bobby-Boy bored senseless.

Wanting to be in the woods.

Playing with his mates...

Yvonne saying, 'Table dancing.'

Bobby-Boy saying, 'You dance on tables?'

Yvonne saying, 'Table-*side* dancing... we are not allowed within three feet of the customers.'

'So, that's all? Dancing?'

'You want to hear this?'

'Only asking.'

'Well, don't.'

Then: 'We get ten pounds, minimum. Each dance lasts two and a half minutes, the length of one song, anything over that is faded out. Could be R&B, soft rock... whatever. I'm a slow dancer, some of the other girls are really fast.'

'And you like doing this?'

'I like the dancing... and I like the exercise. It's long hours, but, the money is good. It can get stressful, sometimes.'

'How long is long hours?'

'Eight-thirty to three-thirty am.'

'Jesus! You're dancing all that time?'

'Not all the time. I like it well enough. You get to meet some interesting people.'

'Like the weatherman?'

Yvonne saying, 'I don't see him any more.'

Bobby-Boy saying, 'That should matter to me?'

Wondering if he could smoke.

Didn't look that kind of place.

Spotting the NO SMOKING signs, one behind the food counter, one on the door as you came in, Bobby-Boy thinking, 'Oh, fuck it!'

Yvonne saying, 'He was in with a crowd from work.'

'And the women were all wearing those diabolical dresses, like they wear when they're reading the weather?'

'It was a stag do... someone on the production team was getting married.'

Then: 'They have to be careful what they wear, you know, so they don't clash with the back-projection. It's not as easy as it looks... that map of Great Britain and Ireland, them pointing, saying, sunny spells in the south, heavy rain expected over Scotland, they can't actually see a thing.'

'Gary tell you all this?'

'You're taking the piss.'

'Would I do that?'

'Just don't.'

Bobby-Boy saying, 'Where was this... what club?'

Yvonne saying nothing.

Then: 'Pink Flamingo. I danced at Stringfellows before that. You had to pay *him* for your pitch – to dance there – did you know that? Now, table-side dancing clubs are opening up all over.'

'Regular growth industry.'

Then: 'You ever see that old Billy Wilder film, *Kiss Me Stupid*?

Dean Martin says to Kim Novak, hands all over her knees, "What's a joint like this doing in a nice girl like you?" '

'What are you trying to say?'

'You don't think that's funny?'

'Watch my face.'

Then: 'My mum and dad died eighteen months ago, car crash in Spain, head-on collision with a tourist coach going the other way... you probably saw it in the papers.'

Bobby-Boy wanting that cigarette.

Badly.

Yvonne saying, 'I was all set for university, media studies, Exeter, year off first to travel round the world. Suddenly, none of that was important.'

'What was important?'

'What was important?'

Thinking about it.

Then: 'Nothing was important.'

Bobby-Boy thinking, Fuck it!

Lighting a cigarette.

Hearing the voice, from a distance, slightly camp.

'Excuse me, sir! Sir, excuse me!'

7

Aurelie wearing only a stretch-denim embroidered top, laying on the kitchen table, Winston standing, supporting her legs, one hand hooked beneath the crook of each of her knees, pushing forward with his pelvis, aware of Aurelie's angular fragility, saying, 'How does this feel?'

Aurelie saying, 'Like I'm a wheelbarrow.'

'You don't like it?'

'It's fine.'

Then: 'Tell me about tattoos.'

'Now?'

'Right now... but, don't stop.'

Winston saying, 'You afraid?'

'Of what?'

'That I'll come too soon.'

'The tattoos… just tell me about the tattoos.'

Aurelie staring at the ceiling.

The light fitting.

Polished aluminium with a counter-weight, on a cord, hanging from the ceiling rose. Sophie had bought it from Ikea. Sophie bought *everything* from Ikea. The light on… Aurelie, her eyes fixed on its brightness, feeling Winston move inside her…

The ring.

Jesus!

Fuck!

The ring.

Aurelie never felt anything like this before in her life.

Winston saying, about the tattoos, 'There are five basic styles… they're on sheets called flashes. You pick what you want done from the flashes.'

Aurelie saying, 'Tell me about it.'

Closing her eyes against the light.

Purple circles branded on her retina.

Winston saying, 'Japanese… samurai, dragons, koi carp.'

'Ah-huh.'

'Tribal.'

'Huh!'

'Maori… swirls and patterns, designed to suit the body.'

'Yes!'

'Celtic… bands and bangles, lots of interwoven patterns, like a wicker carpet beater.'

'Ow!'

'Did I hurt you?'

'Don't stop.'

'What?'

'That's four.'

'No… that's three.'

Winston seeing where Aurelie might have got confused.

Saying, 'Tribal *is* Maori… the swirls and patterns.'

Aurelie saying, 'OK… four! Four!'

'Trad… traditional.'

'Winston!'

'Based on Sailor Jerry, '20s designs. Hearts, daggers, "I love Mother", that kind of shit.'

'Oh, fuck!'

'Modern… wacky stuff. Bugs Bunny… whatever, you name it.'

'Jes-us!'

Aurelie opening her eyes.

Lifting her head.

Saying to Winston, 'You through?'

'You don't know?'

'Why did you stop?'

Behind her, Sophie standing in the kitchen door, been to Sainsbury's, plastic carrier bag in each hand, weight biting into her fingers, dropping the carrier bags at her feet, one of them falling over, carton of Assam tea bags, three leeks in a polythene bag, tumbling to the floor.

Sophie saying, 'Oh, God! I'm sorry.'

Thinking, Why am I sorry?

This is *my* house.

Saying, to Aurelie, 'Aren't you going to introduce me to your friend?'

chapter five

'Make something work!'

1

Bobby-Boy, Charlie Paul and Dennis 'The Diceman' Lightfoot in Bobby-Boy's BMW 3 Series, Charlie in the back, leaning forward between the two front seats, creak of new leather trim as he shifted his weight, instrument panel glowing pale green in the darkness of the car's interior, Bobby-Boy saying, 'Buy a toothbrush, will you, Charlie?' Charlie wondering how the BMW's 'sat-nav' system – whole fucking planet to chose from – could know they are parked up in Turnham Green Terrace, out front of Costa's Fish Bar & Grill, Costa's son, between serving customers, seeing Bobby-Boy's motor, giving them the nod from behind the plate glass window of his old man's chippy. Charlie sinking back into the upholstery, looking out across the terrace, opposite side, parade of shops – deli's, restaurants, Blockbuster Video – Club 67 down the unlit alleyway, the alleyway lined with industrial waste-bins, the industrial waste-bins reeking of Indian and Chinese takeaway, Cajun ribs, Beryl telling them, one time, that the club building was a converted motor repair work-shop – before that, stables – Charlie, not giving a fuck about any of that, wanting this to be done, get across there, get a drink inside him.

A large one.

Could still hear Toyah, outside the health complex, Sing My

Body Electric, saying, 'You would have to be crazy, Charlie... get on the wrong side of Winston.'

Charlie not able to picture Winston and Toyah together.

The image too painful.

Bobby-Boy giving Dennis the once-over on the new motor – Xenon headlamps, Charlie not heard that one before – then getting down to business.

Clarice Cliff.

Original Bizarre.

Circa 1928.

Dennis 'The Diceman' Lightfoot saying, 'You would not believe it, early '80s, you could still pick up this stuff for a fiver, any Oxfam shop. Last year, Christies, a centrepiece called *The Age of Jazz* – designed to sit on the mantelpiece, next to the radio – went for thirteen thousand, eight hundred pounds. Earlier this year, May Avenue pattern tea set fetched another thirteen thousand.'

Bobby-Boy saying, 'I like what I'm hearing.'

'Conical sugar sifter... you could expect two thousand.'

'So, the news is good?'

'Not that good.'

'Disappoint me, Dennis.'

'Six.'

'Six?'

Dennis 'The Diceman' saying, 'Less my usual commission.'

Twenty-five per cent.

Bobby-Boy saying, 'I'm looking at four and a half?'

Charlie Paul, checked out the price of Bobby-Boy's BMW 3 Series, twenty-seven thousand, five hundred on the road, four and a half grand for an afternoon's work, no wonder Bobby-Boy could afford the motor, thinking, Fuck is he complaining about?

The Diceman saying, 'It's not easy out there, Bobby-Boy. If you think you could do better?'

Bobby-Boy saying, 'We've been doing business a long time, Dennis.'

'Take it or leave it, Bobby-Boy.'

'Why do I feel I'm contributing to your retirement fund?'

78

'Consider it a privilege.'

'I'm not a fucking charity.'

Charlie Paul thinking, Tell me about it.

Saying: 'Do we have to go through this shit every fucking time?'

Bobby-Boy saying, 'Shut the fuck up, Charlie.'

Dennis saying, 'Bobby-Boy?'

'Five-five... net.'

'Five?'

Bobby-Boy, checking his off-side wing mirror for traffic, opening the driver's door, looking over his shoulder at Charlie, saying, 'Fuck it.'

Then: 'Must be your shout, Charlie.'

2

David, his glass still a quarter full, thinking, I don't *need* another pint, I *want* another pint.

There is a difference.

A big difference.

Pushing back his seat, standing to go to the bar, saying, 'Whoops!' Lifting his glass from the table – more left than he had realised – thinking, Best clear the decks... emptying the glass, a loud voice saying, 'State of that cunt... pissed as a fart.' David not wanting to look around, see who it was they were talking about... you needed to steer clear of drunks, *never* catch a drunk's eye, engage him in conversation, bound to be in for the duration.

Eight-thirty pm.

Friday night.

The pub crowded... after-work office drinkers, those still remaining, mixing with the first of the local evening crowd. A poster above the bar, another in the window, both reading: *LIVE MUSIC FROM 9.30! FRANK & JOSIE PLAY ALL YOUR FAVOURITE COUNTRY HITS!* David, never liked country music – even well performed country music – thinking, Whatever happened to Country and *Western*? Who took the 'Western' out of 'Country'? Now, *there* was the title for a hit song... thinking,

Thank Christ! I'll be long gone by nine-thirty... saying to the barman, finally caught his eye, 'Pint of Pride, in a straight.'

Then: 'No! Make that ESB.'

Extra Strong Bitter.

Fuller's.

Five-point-nine per cent alcohol by volume.

Put hairs on your chest.

The barman saying, 'Pint?'

David saying, 'Yes, pint.'

Hadn't he already asked for a pint?

Searching for the right money, handing the barman a five pound note, found it in with his small change, screwed up, saying, 'One for yourself?'

The barman saying, 'That's very nice of you, sir... I'll have it later, if I may?'

Then: 'That will be four-eighty.'

David wanting to say, Drink with me now, or not at all.

Instead, saying, 'Forget the twenty.'

Moving away from the bar.

His place immediately taken.

Thinking: This *has* to be the last one.

Peter waiting back at the house – Arlington Gardens – ready for their 'little discussion'. Last night, David falling down the four stairs between his bedroom and the toilet, four-thirty in the morning, waking up the whole household. Karen, turning on the upstairs hall light, taking her daughter in her arms, saying, 'It's all right, Zöe... nothing to be frightened about. Mr Cornish just had an accident, that's all. Mummy put you back to bed.' Then, to her husband, Peter, standing behind her in the hall – David noticing they were wearing matching towelling dressing gowns – 'I'm not having it, Peter. This is our home... we have a child.' David saying, 'I'm terribly sorry, Karen. You would think I would know those stairs are there by now.' Keeping his face averted. Not wanting Karen and Peter to smell the Bells Whisky. Feeling ridiculous, a middle-aged man acting like a naughty child – oughten he be allowed some dignity? – making excuses to this pompous young couple... Shaker this, Shaker that, his room at the back of the house on the first floor about as comfortable as a monk's cell *and* costing him ninety pounds a week. Peter saying, 'Tomorrow, David, OK? We need to have a little discussion.'

David knowing exactly what Peter's 'little discussion' meant...

Had overheard Peter and Karen talking in the kitchen a few nights earlier, David standing motionless at the top of the first floor stairs – had been about to use the toilet, tip-toeing about the house, as usual, feeling uncomfortable being there, despite the rent he paid. Karen saying, 'Do you know how much we could make on that room through a Japanese Letting Agency? Eighty pounds a night... no strings, no complications, just perfect strangers passing through.'

Peter saying, 'I don't know that I want to live with "perfect strangers" constantly passing through.'

Karen saying, 'What does that mean? That you want David as part of the family?'

Then: 'You're forgetting we don't have my salary, now. We have to make up the difference, somehow.'

Before Karen had finished...

Peter saying: 'Could I ever.'

Karen saying, 'Flavour of the month... the Japanese. Did you know, there's even a Japanese "50p in the pound" shop in Ealing... sells nothing but Japanese goods?'

Then: 'You realise he's an alcoholic?'

David, at first, wondering who she was talking about.

Then thinking, Stuck up bloody bitch!

The nerve!

Peter and Karen Leon.

Peter, the junior partner in a successful architectural group with premises in Barnes, Karen, sacrificed a career in journalism, features editor on *Ecoute* – woman's fashion magazine – to have Zöe in her mid-thirties... still playing a power game, but, in the domestic arena; her house spotless, nothing ever out of place, and this with a three year old running around. David reminded of how his ex-wife, Janet, was equally fastidious, forever wiping down surfaces, cleaning, polishing... Janet's younger sister, Deborah, paying a surprise visit one Sunday morning to their first house, in Sheen – she had been to an all-night party, locally. Looked like something the cat dragged in – Deborah a student at St Martin's School of Art, went out with one of the Rolling Stones before they were famous, free-thinker, proto-feminist, sitting at their kitchen table, drinking coffee, smoking untipped Gauloise, saying to Janet, 'Yes, it's all very *chic*... but, where do you *live*?'

David, at the time, thinking, Never mind, where does Janet live? What about me? Where do I live?

Even then, sensing the dull uniformity of his existence, the dreadful inevitability of it all – his marriage, his career in the civil service – this, years before his affair with Sophie – the one brief spark of rebellion in his life – this, even more years before he blurted it all out to Janet, boastful, even... Janet asking for a divorce, their two daughters now at university, flown the nest, Janet saying it had nothing to do with Sophie, everything to do with his drinking, saying, 'David, if there is a woman out there foolish enough to have you... she is more than welcome.'

No home.

No wife and family.

No job.

And now – it would seem – no Sophie.

David, taking his drink back to where he had been sitting, the chair now occupied, the whole table taken by a noisy group of young men, all with pints of lager, all wearing immaculate white trainers, clean pressed designer jeans, dark T-shirts or sports tops, the T-shirts all with large numbers printed on the front... David, a long time ago, given up trying to work out what was fashionable and what was not – a couple standing apart, but with the group at the table, the boy with cropped shoulder-length blond hair, dark at the roots, rough-knit baggy jumper, looked like that pop star who shot himself – Kurt Cobain – the girl wearing a cream leatherette jacket, tan bell-bottoms, David saying to the girl, 'My day, a coat like that would have been considered naff.'

The boy saying, 'Fuck off, piss-head.'

Then: 'Don't you have a park bench to go to?'

David thinking, How very near the truth.

How perspicacious.

Thinking, The shifting sands of a pub crowd.

Very poetic.

The shifting sands of a pub crowd.

Sophie, on the telephone this afternoon, saying, 'I don't want this, David... it isn't that I'm not ready... I don't want this, full stop.'

David saying, 'Not even friends?'

Sophie saying, 'Oh, David, don't be ridiculous... "friends" is not what this is all about.'

Frank and Josie, the country music duet, setting up in the other bar.

Frank testing the PA.

'One, two... one, two.'

Then a snatch of music.

'Little Green Apples'.

David thinking, Oh, dear God, no!

Saying to the boy, 'There a telephone?'

The boy saying, 'Fuck off and die.'

Then: 'Do it now.'

3

First thing Beryl Ulanowski said when Bobby-Boy and Charlie walked in through the door of Club 67, Charlie wearing grey track bottoms, 'Sorry, Charlie, you can't come in wearing those.'

Jeans... fine.

Track bottoms.

Beryl had a pathological hatred.

Said: 'I wanted to operate a gymnasium, I'd get wall bars installed.'

Bobby-Boy saying, 'Wall bars? Gymnasiums have come a long way since wall bars, Beryl. They got these machines like something off the flight deck of a Star Wars film... pec decks, lat pulldowns, leg curls, leg extensions, shoulder press, calf raises, you name it. And that's without the cardio equipment; stationary bikes, rowing machines, stairmaster.'

'No wooden horse?'

'No wooden horse.'

83

'Spring-board?'

'You're giving away your age, Beryl.'

Beryl saying, 'How come you know so much?'

'I used to lift weights.'

This, after Bobby-Boy had the shit kicked out of him by two gorillas, basement flat, South Ken, Bobby-Boy deciding he should invest in a little extra muscle power, not wanting – ever – to repeat the experience... one of the gorillas saying, 'We could call the police.' The other saying, 'Only... I've got a much better idea.'

Another thing that taught Bobby-Boy.

Always leave yourself a way out.

Bobby-Boy saying to Beryl, 'I could lift two-fifty pounds, no sweat.'

Remembered boasting to Winston, Winston giving him that look, saying, 'Two-fifty pounds is not a lot of iron, Bobby-Boy.'

Beryl, back on the subject of track bottoms, saying, 'They're disgusting... you can see everything a man has got.'

Bobby-Boy ordering the drinks – the usual – scotch on the rocks, scotch and coke, saying, 'No Winston?'

Beryl saying to Charlie, 'Just this one time, Charlie. Find yourself a dark corner. And don't forget... I operate a strict dress code.'

Bobby-Boy saying, 'You have anything else?'

'Anything else, what?'

'Dark corners.'

'Ha-bloody-ha.'

Charlie Paul saying, 'Lots of bars, now, they operate a "no hats" policy.'

Bobby-Boy saying, 'Fuck this got to do with anything?'

'We were talking dress codes, right?'

Then: 'Reason being... hats prevent security cameras picking up customer's faces.'

Beryl saying, 'Charlie, I don't have a "no hats" policy.'

'You don't have security cameras, either.'

Bobby-Boy saying, 'You haven't seen him?'

Then: 'Winston?'

Beryl saying, 'No, I haven't seen Winston, and that suits me fine. I don't like the man... he gives me the creeps.'

Then: 'You know, I asked him about that security chain he has hanging round his neck… I said, "Don't the police ever stop you?" He says, "I tell them I just had my bike stolen." I say, "Yeah, but what is it for?" He says, "For in case my bike turns up." '

Then: 'Weirdo.'

And: 'Or, what?'

Bobby-Boy, drink still untouched, wanting it over, speed-dialling Winston, Winston picking up on the second ring…

Saying, 'Yo!'

Bobby-Boy saying, 'You with anybody?'

'What's it to you?'

'You sound short of breath… thought you might be giving it some to some lucky woman.'

'What's this about?'

Bobby-Boy, aware that Charlie Paul and Beryl are both listening, saying, 'The two grand you owe me.'

'What two grand?'

'The Telecaster?'

'Oh, do fuck off.'

'That was my score, Winston.'

'Are you drunk?'

'What?'

'Talking to me like this.'

'Two grand, Winston… I don't intend walking this one round the block.'

Hearing a woman's voice, 'Who is it? Tell them to fuck off.'

Winston saying, 'Shut up, bitch!'

Then, to Bobby-Boy, 'Some you win.'

Breaking the connection.

Bobby-Boy trying to place the woman's voice.

The mobile… lousy connection.

4

Winston saying, 'That was your husband.'

On the phone.

Toyah saying, 'Bobby-Boy?'

'You have another husband?'

Then: 'That's it, Toyah.'

'What do you mean... "That's it"?'

'That's it... we're through. I don't like the way this is heading.'

Toyah's mouth swollen.

Winston slapping her, open-handed, at first.

Toyah saying, 'Harder! Harder!'

Wrapping her two hands round his... shaping his hand into a fist, saying, 'Do it!'

Toyah, now, saying, 'That's it? You fuck me all afternoon without saying a word, then, you say, "That's it"?'

Winston dressing, his back to Toyah, the American bald eagle, the sidewinder, the Harley-Davidson motorcycle, the snow-capped mountains and the flames, all disappearing beneath his crisp white T-shirt.

Winston saying, 'Johnny Depp had WINONA FOREVER changed to WINO FOREVER when he split with Winona Ryder.'

Then: 'Johnny Depp says, "I look at tattoos as a permanent commitment to an experience that you want to remember." '

Toyah saying, 'What does *that* mean?'

'All things change.'

'Yeah, apart from male bullshit.'

Winston saying, 'There's somebody else.'

'Why should I *give* a fuck?'

Then: 'Sharing is no problem.'

Winston, not thinking of Aurelie.

Thinking of her mother...

Sophie.

The way she looked at him from the kitchen door.

Winston backing away from the table, from Aurelie, zipping his fly, buckling his belt, no idea what to say, Sophie, smiling, saying, 'When you two are quite through, I'll put a kettle on, make a cup of tea.'

This woman... old enough to be his mother.

Toyah saying, 'Winston? Hello?'

Then: 'So, who is this paragon of womanhood, she can claim all your attention?'

Winston, not bothering to explain.

Not sure he knew, himself.

Thinking, The fuck!

Am I losing it... or, what?

Saying, 'I'm through with bald... you think a Mohawkan will suit me?'

Toyah saying, 'Go fuck yourself.'

5

David stumbling on the porch step, not seeing it in the dark, thinking, Why did I do that? This kind of house, there is *always* a porch step... light on in the downstairs bay window, was there somebody home, or, was it just a precaution against burglars? Realising he had no idea of Sophie's social life, did she go out much in the evening, did she take evening classes? Ten-fifteen, she could even be in bed, already... then, thinking, Or, could there be another man? Was that the reason? It would certainly explain why she had rejected him.

How long had Jim been dead?

Two years?

Time enough.

David, ringing the bell, realising, Oh Christ! He could be here with her, now... what a bloody fool I would look. The door opening, woman in her late twenties, attractive in a waif-like, bulimic fashion – David could see her as a model... those sunken eyes, hollow cheeks, heroin-chic, isn't that what they called it? – the woman saying, 'What?'

David suddenly realising, saying, 'Aurelie?'

Aurelie, back-lit by the hall light, David seeing everything through the nightdress – whatever – she was wearing, saying, 'The last time I saw you, you must have been nine years old.'

Aurelie saying, 'I expect I've changed a bit, since then.'

'Lady Margaret's Primary School.'

Aurelie saying, 'Fiona Cornish's dad.'

Then: 'You were screwing my mother.'

'Well...'

Then: 'You knew that?'

'*Everybody* knew that… except Jim, of course.'

David saying, 'Yes, I was sorry to hear about your father.'

'Is that why you're sniffing around, now, after all this time… because you heard my dad was dead?'

'That's not…'

Aurelie turning away, calling up the hallway stairs, 'Mother! There's an old flame here to see you!' Then, to David, 'She was in the bath but she's out, now,' and, 'I should tuck your shirt in, you look a mess.' Aurelie leaving David standing on the doorstep, the front door wide open, going back into the living room. David could hear the television as the front room door was opened and then closed… an explosion, another explosion, machine-gun fire – is that what they still called them, machine-guns? – a voice shouting above the cacophony, 'Motherfucker!' Another voice screaming, 'Go! Go! Go!' David thinking, Mindless Hollywood rubbish. Christ! Did they have to be *so* banal? Seeing Sophie's feet first – bare – then her legs, descending the stairs, Sophie, still half-way down, leaning forward and down to see who it was at the front door… David thinking, How many 'old flames' *were* there in Sophie's life?

Sophie wearing a kimono, satin black, with fire-breathing dragons embroidered in gold and crimson red, hair tied back, coming down the hall, now, Sophie saying, 'Oh, David.'

As if she had been bitterly disappointed.

Then: 'You should *not* be here.'

David saying, 'That's a fine greeting.'

'David, how many more times?'

David saying, 'Can I come in? Talk?'

Sophie saying, 'You smell like a brewery.'

Then: 'What would be the point?'

Then: 'Really?'

David saying, 'I'm having trouble where I live… I can't go back like this.'

'But, it's all right to come here?'

'You would be doing me an enormous favour.'

Sophie saying, 'Don't do this to me.'

'Do what?'

'Include me in your life... make me responsible.'

'It isn't like that.'

'It is *exactly* like that.'

David, then, saying, 'At least, let me use your toilet... my bladder is bursting.'

Sophie saying, 'Oh, David.'

Standing aside, saying, 'Top of the stairs on the right... and don't miss the bowl.'

David, in the hall, now, at the foot of the stairs, turning to Sophie, saying, 'Sophie, my whole life is a mess... a failure.'

Sophie saying, 'Don't go pathetic on me. I can't take pathetic.'

6

Toyah, head buried beneath the sheets, teasing the loose tooth, enjoying *that* pain, but not the pain of the split lip. Bobby-Boy undressing, through the covers she could hear him hopping on one leg, getting a sock off – the day he felt he was getting old, Bobby-Boy would sit down to take his socks off – Bobby-Boy saying, 'I like to keep it simple... anybody fucks with me, I fuck right back with them.'

Down to his jockey shorts.

Calvin Klein... white.

Toyah could almost *hear* Bobby-Boy thinking... Take them off?

Or, leave them on.

Toyah saying, 'Winston?'

Bobby-Boy saying, 'Too fucking right, Winston.'

Toyah saying, 'You worry me, Bobby-Boy.'

'How's that?'

'You?'

Then: 'Going up against Winston Capaldi?'

'It's not what you do, Toyah... it's what you convince the other side you are *prepared* to do. Any con will tell you that. Politicians call it brinkmanship.'

'You don't think Winston knows this?'

'That depends.'

Toyah saying, 'There's one big difference, Bobby-Boy.'

'What's that?'

Bobby-Boy pulling back the covers to get into bed.

Toyah, seeing he had decided to take his jocks off, living in hope, Toyah saying, 'Winston doesn't need to bluff.'

Bobby-Boy saying, 'The fuck happened to your face?'

Toyah, about to say, Swing door... the health complex.

Instead, saying nothing.

Couldn't be asked.

chapter six

'Someone in the middle!'

1

Sophie drifting in and out of sleep, fighting the nightmare of consciousness, sleep the seductive *faux* reality in which the man in her bed, pressing his body into her back, his hands caressing her breasts, her stomach, her thighs, taking her shoulder – wanting her to roll into his embrace, open her legs to his tumescence – was her husband, Jim... alive, fit, well; come to her in the early hours of the morning, travelling through the night, as he often did, The Crunch reduced to playing small club gigs up and down the country, the band held together – Jim's words – by bad debt and gaffer tape, Sophie knowing that, tomorrow, over breakfast, he would narrate the usual litany of disaster, each disaster, in itself, no longer unique, commonplace... There were fifty-six punters in and fifty-two of them were on the support band's guest list; the promoter fucked up, it was a heavy metal gig, full of bikers, all screaming for "Freebird", we were lucky to get out of there alive; the PA guy was a complete wanker, we sounded like a pile of shite; Davy was totally out of it on arrival, couldn't keep time if we'd shoved a Rolex up his arse; third number in, the fight broke out...'

And, occasionally.

Just occasionally.

'Fucking great... reminded me why I still do it.'

Sophie hating the good gigs.

Wanting it to be over.

The faded aspirations.

The dreams.

Tired of seeing Jim suffer.

If she had only known, then, the *real* suffering that lay ahead...

Sophie, in the darkness, feeling him enter her from behind – Jim liked to do that, when they were being spoons... called it a lazy shag. Sophie saying, 'You're not with the band, now. You know I hate it when you talk like that' – aware of his size, reminded of the first time she had slept with David, surprised at how big he was compared to Jim... his arms tight around her, whispering, saying, 'You know this is right, Sophie... how could anything that feels this good not be right?'

Only half-waking when Jim came home.

Secure in his presence.

Comforted by his return.

Sophie thinking, How can this be Jim?

Jim is dead.

Remembering that she had allowed David to sleep on the downstairs sofa – the house, with only two bedrooms, now, the builders having knocked through the existing bathroom, combined it with the back-bedroom. Sophie, still unsure of the wisdom of the renovation. Suppose she made contact with her abandoned son? What if he came home to her after all these years? Where would he sleep? – allowing David to stay, against all her instincts, knowing she should have stood her ground, insisted he left.

Oh, Christ!

Jim would be so angry at her stupidity...

Like the time he found her letter to the National Children's Adoption Agency – this in 1977, the year before the agency collapsed – Jim saying, 'What do you think you are doing? *I* don't have a say in this? The boy's natural father? He might not even know he is adopted... did you ever stop to think of that?'

Coming awake.

An involuntary 'Oh!' escaping her lips.

David mistaking her cry as one of pleasure...

Not despair.

Repugnance.

Humiliation.

Moving faster, now, choking Sophie in his embrace, still moving as he came, crying out, saying, 'Oh, Sophie!' Then, whispering close to her ear, 'Sophie, my sweet, sweet darling.'

Kissing the nape of her neck.

As if they were lovers.

Sophie crying into her pillow.

Making no sound.

David, after a few moments, squeezing her gently, saying, 'I love this house... it's so warm, so lived in.'

Then...

Chuckling.

'You can always tell a '60s woman... she can't bear to throw away any colour supplements.'

2

Bobby-Boy and Charlie Paul, drinking lukewarm tea from polystyrene cups – Bobby-Boy's lid marked with a cross, three sugars – parked up in Charlie's C-reg Polo, Charlie behind the wheel, Railton Crescent, fifty yards down and across the road from the three storey detached corner house... Norman Shaw design, red-brick double-frontage, bay windows, first floor balcony, windowed turret, Bobby-Boy thinking, Million and a half of anybody's money.

Charlie Paul saying, 'You think... all the ways there are of making money.'

Bobby-Boy saying, 'Right, Charlie. There was an ad in the *Gazette* last week. In-store Father Christmas, half days, seven days a week, age between forty and sixty-five, successful applicant may tend towards a stout disposition... two-fifty a week.'

Then: 'I thought of you straight away.'

Charlie saying, 'Stout disposition?'

'Fat, Charlie.'

'I know what it means... you saying I have a weight problem?'

'Charlie, you have all *kinds* of problems.'

The house owned by an eccentric.

Confirmed bachelor in his early sixties.

Maintained and drove a 1949 Armstrong Siddley Convertible.

How Bobby-Boy got the word... postal subscription to all the antiques and collectors' magazines. Lewis Beck, humorous bastard – young postie gave Bobby-Boy the information – saying, 'Perhaps, that's what he collects... antiques and collectors' magazines.' Bobby-Boy thinking, Paper-weights, thimbles, 78s, glove and sock darners, cigarette cards, tea pots, porcelain pigs?

It's what made the job interesting.

Could be any fucking thing.

Then, indulging himself.

Thinking: Royal Doulton figurines.

Wouldn't *that* put a smile on The Diceman's face?

Charlie Paul saying, 'Anyway, that's work... I'm not talking about work.'

'What *are* you on about, Charlie?'

Winding down his window.

Dropping the polystyrene cup into the gutter.

Charlie saying, 'Bubble-wrap, for example.'

'Bubble-wrap?'

'How many sheets of bubble-wrap do you think get used every second of every day? You invented bubble-wrap, you would be a rich man.'

Then: 'Or, you can make good money marrying immigrants. Two thousand, five hundred for every time you say, "I do". The Registry Office never cross-references, no way you could ever get caught... of course, it helps if you're a woman.'

Bobby-Boy thinking about the score.

Thinking: Goes off to work at eight-thirty, cleaner comes in at nine. She's out by eleven, except on Thursdays, when she leaves at one o'clock.

Laundry?

Hoovering?

Top to bottom?

Whatever... he got back at six-thirty.

Five days a week.

Regular as clock-work.

Charlie Paul saying, 'Look at Bill Gates, invented the silicon chip... the richest man in recorded history.'

Bobby-Boy saying, 'Bill Gates did not invent the silicon chip.'

Thinking...

No animals.

No security.

Piece of piss.

Watching as the cleaning lady came out of the front door, handbag in one hand, full black plastic sack in the other, putting down the black plastic sack to close the front door – bog-standard Yale, she just pulled the door shut – then, depositing the black plastic sack in the brick-built rubbish container concealed behind a stand of azalea.

Bobby-Boy saying to Charlie, 'I should seriously consider the red suit and whiskers.'

Then: 'OK... let's do it.'

3

Sophie, alone in her bed, picturing – if she rolled over – that Jim would be there, sleeping... not rolling over, not wanting to shatter the illusion. Sun streaming in through the bedroom window, the weather forecasters already predicting this would be the warmest and driest autumn in fifty years... remembering the time Jim had come home so angry he had to wake her, four-thirty in the morning, saying, 'Fucking promoter, right? Says to me over the phone – this is months ago – not, "How much?" or, "What are we looking at?" No, the fucker says, "How much for?"

'So, I say, "Four hundred."

'He *thinks* I say, "For a hundred."

'Can you imagine?

'Preston and back... how many miles is that?

'Twenty-five quid each.

'Before petrol.

'Drinks.

'A meal.'

Sophie saying, 'Did you get the money?'

'Like fuck did we get the money.'

Then: 'He called his club "The Pitz". Can you imagine?'

Next day, carrying his breakfast plate from the cooker to the kitchen table, Jim's hand went into spasm, his breakfast ending up all over the floor. Jim saying, 'How the fuck did I manage that?'

Fried eggs.

Bacon.

Tomatoes.

Toast.

Sophie wondering, later, Was it Jim's anger, his tiredness, his frustration that had triggered that first attack?

Neither of them, at the time, any idea what it meant.

Sophie saying, 'Sit in the other room, read the paper. I'll clear this up, cook you another breakfast.'

Jim...

A taut bow-string.

Saying: 'Bollocks! Since when have I asked you to be my slave?'

Sophie throwing back the covers.

Scrambling from the bed.

Couldn't abide the thought of being in it – her *own* bed – one moment longer.

4

Most of the rooms empty.

Or, full of junk.

Furniture piled up...

Covered in dust sheets.

From the very top room, the turret, Bobby-Boy could see the Thames, above the roof-tops, winding towards Hammersmith Bridge. In the street below, Charlie's Volkswagen Polo, Charlie, hopefully, ready to call him on the mobile, anything untoward occurred. Bobby-Boy sticking to his usual modus operandum, working down from the top to the bottom. On the ground floor, front room to the left of the hall stairs, there was a neatly made single bed, set against the wall furthest away from the window, a throw rug – seen better days – in front of the bed, a china chamber pot underneath the bed... not much else, except a framed Charlie Bubbles mounted above the open fire-place, a paperback novel, *The Mauritius Command* by Patrick O'Hara, on the floor next to the bed.

Bobby-Boy checking behind the picture for a wall safe.

Thinking, Well... if you can't be bothered, don't bother.

Blank wall staring back at him.

The room opposite, other side of the hall at the front, was a living room with a twenty-four inch colour television set, bookcase full of books, mainly paperback, all fiction, a dresser, table in the bay window, pile of magazines between the sofa and an easy chair; Bobby-Boy noticing *FHM, Loaded*, some top shelf stuff – *Playbird, Escort, Men's World, Adult Cinema* – as well as copies of *Antiques Collector, Classic Cars*, and *Collect It!* On the table in the window was a copy of yesterday's *Mail On Sunday*. On the dresser were a number of inscribed silver cups and photographs in ornate silver or gold frames. The photographs were all in black and white and showed the mark in a dress suit with tails and a woman with tightly permed dark hair wearing a low-cut sequined taffeta gown, the photographs taken at various ballroom dancing events up and down the country. There was a framed press cutting, the two of them swirling around a dance floor, a caption underneath reading, *'Peter Sykes and June Anne Fellowes, Southern Area Regional Ballroom Dancing Champions, Worthing Assembly Halls, August, 1974.'*

Bobby-Boy wondering what happened to June Anne Fellowes.

Whether their relationship had remained strictly professional.

Dumping the dresser drawers out on the floor.

The bottom drawer, cardigans, jumpers, – all V-neck – shirts.

The middle drawer, Y-fronts, vests – *string* vests, for fuck's sake! – socks, all grey, all one hundred per cent pure wool.

The two smaller drawers at the top of the dresser yielded braces – no clip-ons – cufflinks, scarves, a shoe horn, a cigar box full of buttons, a traveller's sewing kit, three petrol lighters – none of them working – a clothes brush, a box of drawing pins, an open packet of assorted elastic bands, an old fountain pen, a shoe box containing bills that dated back ten years, all marked paid... all marked with the date on which they had been paid.

No cash.

No switch cards, credit cards, cheque books.

Nothing negotiable.

Bobby-Boy then emptying the book shelves, shaking each book by its spine before discarding it... Bobby-Boy always amazed at how many people preferred to keep their life savings on a book shelf rather than in a bank.

Drawing another blank.

Thinking, Peter Sykes– you tight old bastard.

Then – in the back sitting room, cut off from the living room by the original sliding wooden dividers – Bobby-Boy found the collection.

Row of shoe boxes, stacked against the wall, Bobby-Boy opening one of the shoe boxes, taking out a bag... there must have been at least fifty in each box. Written on the outside of the bag, it said: *'SUN AIRE LINES'*, then, in smaller print, *'For motion sickness and other emergencies.'* The second bag was *'AIR AFRIQUE'*. It had a picture of a woman giving birth, Bobby-Boy wondering if that's what the first bag meant by *'other emergencies.'* A third bag – Bobby-Boy delving down into the shoe box, picking at random – read: *'TACA INTERNATIONAL FLIGHTS'*, the accompanying copy, aiming to reassure, saying, *'Even veteran travellers are subject to occasional motion sickness.'*

The last bag Bobby-Boy pulled out of the shoe box went straight to the point...

It read: *SIC-SAC.*

The original motion sickness bag.

The word *'SIC-SAC'* framed by two cartoon goblins, one chasing the other.

Bobby-Boy thinking, Well, fuck you, too, Peter Sykes.

Picking up one of the shoe boxes.

Would be a laugh to show them round at the club... Beryl, especially, would find it all very amusing.

Then, thinking, Fuck it!

Putting the box back.

Why spoil the mad fucker's collection?

5

Winston running his hand through the fuzz, a four inch band of dark stubble, cleaving his otherwise bald dome, from front to back.

Charlie Paul – drinking a beer, too early in the day for scotch – saying, 'Looks like you popped up out of a manhole at the wrong moment.'

Then: 'Tyre track.'

Then: 'Get it?'

Beryl laughing.

Got the joke before the explanation.

Winston saying, 'I'm growing a Mohawkan.'

Charlie saying, 'You mean Mohican?'

Winston staring at Charlie.

Then, saying, 'No, I mean Mohawkan. Mohawkans ate Mohicans for breakfast... Mohawkan means, "People who eat people".'

Beryl saying, 'Charming.'

Winston pissed off.

Been on the mobile to Eric Holtz all morning, trying to arrange another meeting before he left town, Eric staying at the Metropole, the receptionist telling Winston, 'I'm sorry, sir, but, Mr Holtz does not appear to be answering.'

Winston saying, 'Is he in his room?'

The receptionist saying, 'As far as I know, sir... he hasn't checked out.'

Every fucking time.

Now, Club 67, lunchtime, hoping to make contact with Bobby-Boy, Charlie telling Beryl about the score – air sickness bags – the two of them laughing, Winston not about to find *anything* amusing this morning, saying, to Charlie Paul, 'Bobby-Boy coming in?'

Charlie saying, 'Why don't you call him?'

Then, to Beryl, 'Ballroom dancer, right? Collected sick bags.'

Winston going out into the alley.

Punching in Bobby-Boy's number.

Bobby-Boy answering, Winston saying, 'I don't want there to be any bad blood between us.'

Bobby-Boy saying, 'Bit late for that.'

'What if I offered you a grand… finder's fee?'

'Do fuck off.'

Then: 'You been in touch with Holtz?'

'Who told you that?'

'Little birdy.'

'Yeah, little birdy with a fat gut, bald head and a personal hygiene problem.'

Bobby-Boy laughing, saying, 'You should know, by now, Charlie Paul knows fuck all about anything.'

Winston saying, 'You know Holtz?'

Bobby-Boy saying, 'Hold on… I need to make a right.'

Then: 'OK, I'm with you.'

Then: 'Eric Holtz? All his clients are private collectors. He deals in art work, antique jewellery, first editions… anything too well known to reappear on the open market.'

Then: 'You took the Telecaster to him?'

'Why not?'

'No doubt, Eric pissed himself laughing.'

Then: 'You're out of your league, Winston. Stick to car boot sales, why don't you?'

Back at the bar, Winston asking Beryl for an OJ, no ice, Charlie saying, 'You get through?'

Winston saying, 'Fuck is it to you?'

Thinking, One day, Charlie.

One day very soon.

6

Sophie had the bathroom of her dreams.

A bathroom to die for…

On the first floor, straight ahead from the hallway stairs, the existing bathroom and toilet combined with the back bedroom and part of the upstairs hall; the bath, Victorian claw foot, cast-

100

iron with original brass fittings, standing on a central riser, the riser finished in limestone and inlaid mosaic tiling. The floor was polished pine with oriental throw rugs, the walls pale cream with apricot trim. There were wicker plant stands trailing spider plants, fern and ivy – one stand neatly obscuring the toilet bowl in the right hand corner – a Lloyd-Loom chair beside the bath, mahogany towel rack, the bath towels in rich spice colours... terracotta, mulberry and berry... two Matisse prints, *The Red Studio* and *The Moroccans*, in green lacquered frames, the frames from Ikea – there had to be *something* from Ikea – along with the wall-mounted light fittings in blown opal and the central pendant lamp in lacquered steel and frosted glass.

The money coming from a windfall.

The Tom Jones cover of Jim's song, 'Maybe Tomorrow', featuring in an American crime noir film, *Gallows Talk*, with Stanley Tucci and Jennifer Lopez, the film a surprise box-office hit, the compilation CD of the soundtrack, featuring mostly obscure '60s singles – the film's director showing what a smart-arse he was – charting in the States.

Sophie's builder saying, 'Famous, was he... your husband?'

Then: 'You want, we can move the washing machine, plumb it in up here?'

Sophie saying, 'I think not... I want this room to be perfect.'

Ignoring the first question.

Aurelie, taking in the Victorian bath, the Matisse prints, the Ikea light fittings, saying, 'Just exactly what century are we meant to be in?'

Then: 'We live in a rubbish tip for two months for this? A bathroom with no shower? How am I supposed to wash my hair?'

Sophie, soaking in the bath, now.

Aurelie coming in without knocking.

Saying: 'Did you see my razor?'

Then: 'One day I'll be able to afford a wax.'

Sophie saying, 'Leg waxing causes inverted hairs... inflamed follicles. Did you know that?'

Then: 'Aurelie, I want us to change rooms.'

'Change rooms?'

'Bedrooms.'

Aurelie thinking of all those things she couldn't bring herself to do in her own bedroom, her childhood breathing down her neck, her own sweet innocence watching over her shoulder she so much as thought of Winston between her legs.

'You'd be happy in the smaller room?'

'I know you use my bedroom... I'm not blind. Besides, there is too much of Jim in there. I can't sleep.'

'Too much of Jim never bothered you before.'

'Perhaps, it's time to move on.'

'David?'

'What about David?'

'You two an item?'

Aurelie surprised when Sophie burst into tears.

Then, Sophie saying, 'Aurelie, I feel so dirty.'

7

Bobby-Boy ringing Yvonne, stuck in traffic, Sutton Court Road, thinking, Cable and fucking Wireless, saying to Yvonne, when she picked up, 'It's me.'

'Me?'

'Bobby-Boy.'

'I hate it when people say that, "It's me".'

Then: 'Even worse, when they say, "Only me". You think, Well, if it's only you, why bother calling me in the first place?'

Bobby-Boy saying, 'Can we meet up?'

'I know what this is... you are starting to see me as a missed opportunity.'

'I think my wife is fucking around.'

'What makes you think that?'

'She's got this tattoo.'

'Tattoo?'

'Base of her spine—'

'Coccyx.'

'You say so... the weirdest looking bird you'll ever see.'

'Did you know that eighty per cent of armed robbers are tattooed?'

'I'm serious.'

'I'm not into this as a tit-for-tat situation.'

'That's not the way it is… I can talk to you.'

Yvonne saying, 'My role as therapist. It's not a particularly original line, Bobby-Boy… the shoulder to cry on routine.'

Then: 'Did you ever think? You split "therapist" into two words, you get "the rapist"?'

'Why are you giving me a hard time?'

Somewhere ahead, a traffic light changing to green.

Bobby-Boy easing the Beamer forward the length of three cars.

Yvonne saying, 'Because I suspect it might be time *somebody* did… and, because you woke me up. You realise what the time is?'

Bobby-Boy checking the facia.

Saying, 'It's two-fifteen.'

Then: 'How about lunch?'

'Make that breakfast.'

Then: 'Sally-Anne's… off Acton Green?'

'I know Sally-Anne's.'

Yvonne saying, 'Give me an hour.'

Bobby-Boy cutting left into Arlington Gardens, then right towards the High Road, making one more call once he had made it across the traffic and into Chiswick High Road, heading east.

'Hotel Metropole!'

'Eric Holtz?'

'His number is ringing, sir.'

'Thank you.'

Then: 'Eric?'

'Bobby-Boy… how goes it?'

'I owe you.'

'You owe me nothing… what are friends for?'

Then: 'The guitar?'

Bobby-Boy saying, 'Give me seven days.'

8

Winston in a cab, Vauxhall Vectra, going from Club 67 to the flat in Sheen, ten minute drive anywhere but Chiswick, contra-flow

system, temporary lights, bulldozers, earth diggers, drilling rigs...
only last week, some fucker went through a gas main, whole of
the High Road evacuated for twenty-four hours... seeing
Aurelie's mother, Sophie, standing at the bus stop, leaning
forward, saying to the cab driver, 'Pull over.' The cab driver
saying, 'I can't stop here.' Winston saying, 'The fuck you can't
stop here. You see anything else moving?'

Sophie at the curb.

Lost.

Bewildered.

Winston thinking of Haversham.

Adult Psychiatric Wing... juvenile offenders seconded for
'ward maintenance duties.'

'Largactylshuffle,' they called it.

Inmates pumped full of shit so they wouldn't cause any problems...

The cab pulling in beside Sophie.

Winston opening the rear passenger door, saying, 'Can I offer
you a lift?'

Single-decker bus, E3, stuck in the traffic up ahead, level with
Devonshire Road and the Roman Catholic Church. Sophie's bus,
if she was going back to Grove Park... must have just missed it.

Sophie saying, 'It's you.'

Totally out of it.

Winston saying, 'Let me give you a ride home.'

Remembering what Aurelie had said.

Valium?

Librium?

Fuck did it matter?

One of the benzodiazepines.

Sophie saying, 'I'm not going home.'

Then: 'Aurelie is doing the shopping.'

Then: 'Can you imagine... Aurelie doing the shopping?'

Bus, 267, pulling in behind the cab.

Driver sounding his horn.

Elderly women picking up their Sainsbury's shopping bags,
some with the old man still in tow – not dead yet, poor bastard –

hurrying forward to get on the bus, didn't want anybody pushing in ahead of them.

One saying, 'I've waited half an hour for this bus.'

Another saying, 'Shocking, isn't it?'

A third saying, 'Go on... you were in front of that woman.'

Sophie saying, 'You look different.'

Then: 'You're not bald, any more... at least, not completely bald.'

Winston saying, to the cab driver, 'What do I owe you?'

The cabbie saying, 'You just got in.'

Then: 'Minimum fare... two fifty.'

Winston passing the driver three pound coins.

Getting out of the cab.

Saying, to Sophie, 'I'll wait with you.'

Sophie saying, 'There's really no need.'

Then: 'I've been to the police station. You know, they only let you in one at a time? I was going to speak to the constable.'

'Desk sergeant.'

'Sergeant? He looked so young.'

Then: 'I gave up waiting in the end.'

Then: 'Besides, I couldn't imagine telling that young man anything... would have been *far* too embarrassing.'

Winston saying, 'Is it something you can tell me?'

'Seems silly, now.'

'What does?'

'Such a fuss over nothing.'

Winston saying, 'Look... I'll walk you home.'

Then: 'Through the park.'

Then: 'A walk will do you good.'

Sophie saying, 'I don't want to go home.'

'Where *do* you want to go?'

'Anywhere... not home.'

Then: 'What will Aurelie say?'

Winston saying, 'About what?'

chapter seven

'Nice one!'

1

Dennis The Diceman, big wink to Beryl, saying to Charlie –
Charlie just through telling The Diceman about Bobby-Boy's sick
bags – 'I knew a bloke, once, collected "Do Not Disturb" signs
from hotel rooms... pharmaceutical sales rep, spent most of his
time in Third World countries selling suspect drugs to the
natives... each "Do Not Disturb" sign represented some tart he
had knocked off in his hotel room. Never took a sign unless he
had made bona fide usage of it... scrupulous about that, he was.'

Beryl saying, 'A man of integrity... married, was he?'

'Of course, married.'

'Sleazebag.'

Charlie Paul saying, 'So, in actual fact, this collection of "Do
Not Disturb" signs was a coded record of how many women he
had fucked during the course of his travels.'

'In one, Charlie.'

Beryl saying, '"Tart?" "Knocked off?" "Fucked?" What is
this? I'm going to have to introduce a few new house rules around
here with regard acceptable language on my premises.'

Dennis saying, 'Sorry, Sonja... it's just that I always considered
you as one of the boys.'

'Thanks a bunch, Dennis.'

Ignoring the 'Sonja'.

Dennis saying, 'Funniest thing was... his missus never cottoned on. She used to get him to show off his collection to friends when they came round.'

Beryl saying, 'Daft cow.'

Charlie saying, 'So, how many "Do Not Disturb" signs did he have in his collection?'

'Rough count, around two thousand.'

'Two thousand?'

Then: 'He slept with two thousand women?'

'There abouts.'

Charlie repeating, 'Two thousand.'

'At the last count.'

Dennis adding, 'And this not including his wife... plus whoever else he screwed whilst not on his travels.'

Beryl saying, 'Yellow card, Dennis.'

'Screwed?'

'Arguing with the ref.'

Charlie remembering what Bobby-Boy had said to him, the two of them talking about Winston, Charlie saying, 'I just don't get what it is about Winston. Nine out of ten women find him completely repulsive. The other one in ten falls head over heels... worships the very ground he walks on.'

Bobby-Boy saying, 'You don't think one in ten is enough for any man, Charlie?'

Charlie thinking, One in a million would be a fine thing.

Beryl saying, 'Hello, Charlie?'

Then: 'Charlie, hello?'

Dennis The Diceman saying, 'Course, he was in his fifties... two thousand is not an exceptional amount of women by the time you reach your fifties.'

Beryl saying, 'You are a cruel bastard, Dennis.'

Then, to Charlie, 'While I remember... Toyah rang for you, earlier.

Dennis, winking, saying, 'Hello, hello!'

Charlie saying, 'Toyah?'

Then: 'For me?'

Beryl saying, 'I know of no other Charlie Paul.'

'What did she want?'

'She wanted you to join the modern world… buy a mobile.'

Charlie all a-tremble.

Hoping Beryl and Dennis wouldn't notice.

Give him a hard time.

Thinking, Toyah… now, *she* would be enough for any man. You could forget the other one thousand, nine hundred and ninety-nine.

… you had Toyah.

Dennis saying, 'What about you, Charlie? Do you keep score with regard the matter of carnal conquest?'

Beryl saying, 'Carnal conquest?'

Charlie saying, 'Ha-bloody-ha.'

Then, to Beryl, 'This wouldn't be a wind-up, about Toyah ringing?'

Beryl saying, 'Charlie, you must be confusing me with one of the boys.'

2

Winston standing naked in front of Sophie's bedroom dresser, top right-hand drawer wide open, the drawer where Sophie kept all her important documents: birth certificates, Jim's death certificate, passport, mortgage papers, house insurance, life insurance, social security details, bills, receipts, guarantees… Aurelie, by the bed, towelling her hair, still moaning that the house had no shower, wearing a salmon pink mohair tank top – nothing else – the mohair tank top, Marcus's last Christmas present to Aurelie before they split up, a hundred and thirty-five pounds from Ghost, in Notting Hill Gate. Aurelie studying Winston's back, the snow-capped mountains, the flames, knowing there would be no gifts like that in *this* relationship, seeing what he was doing, saying, 'Help yourself, why don't you?'

Then: 'My dad used to laugh at Sophie. He'd say, "House insurance? Life insurance? Why do we need all that crap?" Sophie would say to him, things like, "One of us has got to look to the future," and "Better safe than sorry."'

Then: 'Turned out Sophie was right… about the life insurance.'

And: 'My dad spent his whole adult life paranoid that people would mistake him for a normal human being.'

Winston ignoring Aurelie.

Reading the letter.

Taken from a large buff envelope marked: DEVON '65.

Reading: *While we remain sympathetic to your situation, we must remind you that your original decision was made on the basis of complete confidentiality.*

Reading: *Our primary obligation is to protect the rights of the children concerned. There are adopted adults who do not wish to know their birth mother. There are also those who do not know they are adopted.*

And: *I must advise you that our decision in this matter is final and that we are not able to enter into further correspondence.*

The letter signed, *Donald Bergman, Chairman, Social Services Committee, Hounslow Borough Council.*

The reference: *MALE INFANT/DATE OF BIRTH 4/6/65 (REFERRAL N.C.A.A. 9/10/78)*

There was another letter, this one from Sophie to the West London Natural Parent Support Group, asking for their help, Sophie enclosing a copy of the letter from Hounslow Borough Council. All Winston learnt from the second letter was that NCAA stood for National Child Adoption Association.

Aurelie, behind him, peeling off the mohair tank top.

Pulling back the covers.

Getting into bed.

Saying, 'It's cold in here on my own.'

Winston thinking about his tenth birthday.

Frank and Penny's decision to tell him everything.

Winston saying, 'Did you know you had an older brother?'

Aurelie saying, 'Sure, I knew… lucky escape, right?'

Then: 'So much for the swinging '60s.'

'Were you ever curious?'

'About an older brother…? Oh, come on.'

'I mean, now? Would you like to meet him, now?'

Aurelie thinking, saying, 'Well, maybe, if he was a millionaire… a rich pop star. Something like that.'

109

Winston putting away the letters.

Closing the drawer.

Getting into bed with Aurelie.

Aurelie saying, 'What you did last time... do it again, will you?'

Winston saying, 'You're missing the point.'

'What point?'

'The element of surprise.'

Pushing his finger deep into Aurelie's anus.

Saying, 'You like that?'

Aurelie saying, 'Hey, it's a start.'

Winston surprising himself...

Realising he had wanted to fuck his own mother from the moment he had set eyes on her.

That...

Right now.

He was fucking his own baby sister.

3

Toyah didn't mind Bobby-Boy being a thief.

But...

A cheat?

A *serial* cheat?

That was an entirely different matter.

Standing at the window in the back top floor bedroom, the bedroom converted into a dressing room with a wall-length fitted wardrobe, beechwood with louvred doors and brass fittings, deep shelves for knitwear, multi-level shoe rack – also, in beechwood – a floor to ceiling illuminated mirror, all Toyah needed was a support rail, she could climb into a tutu, practice her *pliés* and *arabesques*. One thing about Bobby-Boy, he never minded spending money if he thought it would keep Toyah happy.

Two empty suitcases open on the floor.

Toyah wondering what she should put in them.

The fitted wardrobe and the shelves full of clothes, most of them she had only ever worn in the changing cubicle... Harvey Nicholls, The Warehouse, Pied à Terre, Kangol, Whistles, Russell & Bromley.

Admitting to herself.

This she would miss.

Looking out of the window onto a grey afternoon, Ravenscourt Park... the promenade with its avenue of poplars, the leaves finally fallen from the branches, the tennis courts, the red clay football pitch, the ornamental gardens, the boating lake and island... there hadn't been a boat on the lake for years, still, anybody local called it the boating lake. Immediately beyond the row of back gardens, The One O'clock Club, the building and fenced-in compound with climbing frames and a sand pit... Toyah wondering if it would have worked out different if she and Bobby-Boy had had kids.

Knowing she no longer *gave* a fuck.

Hearing the phone ring downstairs.

The phone...

Remembering the very first time one of Bobby-Boy's women had rung him at home. The woman – sounded more like a girl than a woman – saying, 'It's Kite... can I speak to Bobby-Boy?'

Toyah saying, 'Ring this number, again, slag, and I'll squeeze your tits like lemons.'

Wondering, after she had put the phone down...

Squeeze your tits like lemons?

What had induced her to come out with something like that?

Saying to Bobby-Boy, later, 'You know a Kite?'

'You mean a cheque?'

'No... a woman.'

Bobby-Boy saying, 'Kite?'

'She rang, earlier... wanted to speak to you.'

Bobby-Boy saying, 'A woman? For me? Kite?'

Then: 'What kind of fucking name is Kite?'

Turning it into a joke.

Saying, 'Kite? What? As in, 'High as a... ?'

And: 'Out of her head, was she?'

Then: 'Course, I don't know any fucking Kite.'

Toyah, finding out, later...

It was Kate.

From Birmingham.

The phone still ringing.

Toyah knowing it was Charlie.

Remembering, now, that primary school teacher – stuck-up bitch – where Charlie had worked as caretaker.

Adriana.

Now, *Adriana* was serious.

Bobby-Boy's usual line, 'It meant nothing' – as if that should mean it also meant nothing to Toyah – replaced by a pathetic helplessness… 'I was obsessed… infatuated. There was nothing I could do about it.'

Exonerating himself from blame.

Culpability.

Toyah holding her index finger – Hitler moustache – beneath her nose, head thrown back, mock-German accent, saying, 'I voss only obeying my prick.'

Not expecting Bobby-Boy to find it funny.

Bobby-Boy saying, 'Toyah, you're not hearing me.'

Toyah saying, 'Oh, I'm hearing you.'

Then: 'Loud and clear.'

Remembering, too, the first time she had opened her legs to Winston…

That weird feeling.

The ring.

Sweet Jesus Christ!

Thinking, Got you, you bastard!

Meaning Bobby-Boy.

Not, Winston.

The phone still ringing.

Bobby-Boy never wanting an answerphone.

Saying, 'It's that important, they'll ring back.'

And: 'The fuck should I help British Telecom double their profits?'

His main concern, that some fuck-wit might leave an incriminating message. Saying to Toyah, 'Old Bill comes calling with a warrant… wouldn't he be amused.'

Toyah descending the stairs.

Taking her time.

The phone, wall-mounted, in the downstairs hall.

Toyah, her mind back on the problem of the two empty suit-cases – what to put in them? – picking up the phone, saying, 'Hello, Charlie.'

Thinking, Forget the LBD… colour is the new black.

4

Robert coming up trumps.

Bobby-Boy saying, 'This is on the up and up, there'll be a drink in it.'

Robert saying, 'No need for that, Bobby-Boy… not after last time. Make up for all the aggravation.'

Bobby-Boy saying, 'Be so daft. I'll look after you, right?'

Robert catching up with Bobby-Boy and Yvonne in Sally-Anne's, Bobby-Boy with one of the Sally-Anne lunchtime specials; liver and bacon, mash, and two veg – boiled greens and carrots – a mountain of food, Yvonne with scrambled eggs on toast, orange juice, both of them with large teas, two sugar. Bobby-Boy, earlier, when they came in, clocking the working stiffs, copy of the *Sun* propped up against the ketchup bottle, shovelling it down like there was going to be no tomorrow, saying, 'You are what you eat, right?' Waiting for the food, window table looking out on the green where the 94 bus turned around, Bobby-Boy telling Yvonne about Toyah's swollen jaw, Toyah refusing to say, one way or the other, how it had happened. Bobby-Boy relieved that the swelling had gone down, saying, 'Can you imagine what the neighbours were thinking?' Then: 'Pity that fucking tattoo couldn't have gone the same way.' Robert and the food arriving together, Bobby-Boy saying, 'Timing… it's what makes the world go round.' Then, seeing Robert's face, gauze bandage taped across his nose, saying, 'Still tender?'

Saying, to Yvonne, 'Fracas with a mutual acquaintance.'

Yvonne saying, 'I'm not dying to meet him.'

Bobby-Boy saying, 'You're right… it *was* a bloke.'

'You think a woman would do something like that?'

'Don't get me started.'

Thinking, Robert's face…

Winston.

Toyah's swollen jaw.

Tattoos… Winston?

Then, thinking, Fuck off!

Paranoid, or what?

Robert telling Bobby-Boy what he had heard his Aunt Jean tell his mother… how Aunt Jean had found the lady she 'did for', Mrs Evangelides, dead in her living room armchair, cup of cold Ovaltine and two digestive biscuits on a tray across her lap, the television – black and white – still on from the previous evening. Aunt Jean finding her when she went in to clean in the morning. Aunt Jean telling Robert's mother Mrs Evangelides had lived on the ground floor, owned the whole house, Grafton Drive, off the Bath Road, let out two rooms, furnished, and a self-contained unfurnished flat on the top floor. Collected her rent in cash every week, plus her state widow's pension and attendance allowance of £102 and small change. Never went out – it was Aunt Jean went to the post office for her pension and attendance allowance – and never spent one penny she didn't need to spend… Robert saying, 'Tight as a rat's arse.' Bobby-Boy saying, 'Your Aunt Jean said that?' Robert saying, 'No, *I* said that.' Had meals on wheels delivered by the social services, wore an overcoat indoors rather than turn on the central heating, thought a colour television was a waste of money, telling Aunt Jean, 'Same programmes as you see in black and white.' Her own telephone a pay-phone.

Didn't have a bank account.

Didn't trust anybody – especially, banks – with her money.

Bobby-Boy saying, 'Didn't have a bank account?'

Robert saying, 'There is a son. He's flying back from New Zealand to take care of the funeral arrangements… sort out the house.'

Bobby-Boy saying to Yvonne, 'It looks as if this afternoon isn't going to happen.'

Yvonne saying, 'Business before pleasure.'

Then: 'Eat your liver and bacon.'

Then, to Robert, 'What did *you* have planned for this afternoon?'

Robert looking at Bobby-Boy.

Blushing.

5

It was Peter Leon asking David if he would prefer lapsang souchong or Earl Grey that really did it for David, Karen Leon standing behind David at the kitchen table – their precious daughter, Zöe, packed off to bed a half hour early – he could almost *feel* the faces Karen was making to her husband behind his back.

Peter saying, 'If you do have a problem, a serious problem, it would make absolute sense to seek counselling. The AA... I'm sure they must have a local branch.'

David wondering about the indefinite article.

How the 'the' prefixing AA made it seem as if Peter was talking about the Automobile Association... deciding against making a crack. Instead, saying – about the tea – 'Assam... don't you have any straight-forward Indian tea? With milk and sugar?'

Adding, 'White sugar.'

Karen saying, 'You know we don't use sugar.'

Then: 'White *or* brown.'

David restricting himself to two pints at lunchtime.

Not wishing to fuel the Leon's malevolent fantasies.

Wanting it to be over.

This 'little discussion'.

Peter saying, 'We just hope that you won't take it personally... it's just we have our daughter to consider. Children of her age are very impressionable.'

David thinking about Sophie.

Why had she been so cool towards him the next morning?

Now, not taking his calls.

The phone remaining unanswered, or, Aurelie saying she was out.

If he knew where he stood with Sophie, then, God willing, he could tell this insufferably self-obsessed couple exactly where it was they could get off.

Karen saying, 'How soon, do you think, would be practicable?'

Peter saying, 'Not that there's any immediate rush... you will need time to sort out alternative arrangements.'

Then: 'Obviously, we're not about to turf you out into the street.'

Karen saying, 'We *would* prefer sooner, rather than later.'

Peter saying, 'And, if you need a reference.'

David saying, 'That's very kind.'

Thinking, *Nimby*.

Not in my back yard.

Open cast mining.

Fast-track rail links with the Continent.

New council estate housing developments.

David reading, only last week, in the local rag, householders in Stamford Brook convening a meeting, objecting to a Notting Hill Housing Trust plan to build a hostel – on the site of a disused children's play area – which would house six schizophrenics.

David laughing when he read it.

Thinking, They should also have been single parent Afro-Carribean lesbians...

With AIDS.

Still unable to accept that the Leons saw him as the personification of undesirable. Saying, to Peter, 'You mentioned a cup of tea?'

Karen saying, 'Oh, Peter. This is hopeless.'

6

Toyah and Charlie Paul in the Thatched House, Paddenswick Road, short walk from Bobby-Boy and Toyah's place in Ravenscourt Road, Toyah with a Bacardi and coke, Charlie a pint of Young's Special – Toyah had avoided Charlie coming into the flat, might have got the wrong idea. Charlie, not sure *what* was going on, thinking, Why did Toyah ring me? Is this like... a date? What is she expecting? Toyah saying, 'Bobby-Boy will never come in here... it's always full of coppers from the police section house over the road.'

Charlie saying, 'How could I fail to notice?'

Thinking, Gone were the days of the grey trousers, smart

crease, polished lace-up black shoes... even off-duty cops had joined the jeans and trainers revolution.

Still wore size tens, though.

Still tell they were cops.

Toyah saying, 'Relax, Charlie, I'm not going to eat you.'

Charlie thinking, Chance would be a fine thing.

Saying, 'Did you know, the Scottish Highlands has the highest suicide rate in the whole of Europe. They reckon it's lack of light and because the locals have nothing else to do all day except drink themselves stupid.'

'Really.'

'Plus, they get a lot of tourists up from the south. Something to do with Inverness station being the furthest you can travel north on a train.'

Then: 'There's one of those suspension bridges near Inverness. Always some fucker or other jumping off it.'

Toyah saying, 'Bobby-Boy told me you like a conversation.'

Then: 'You have a cigarette paper stuck to your throat.'

Charlie saying, 'Oh, shit.'

Soon as he had spoken to Toyah on the phone, Charlie had gone back to the flat, Addison Gardens, council block next to Hammersmith Town Hall – still called it his mum's flat, despite she had been dead ten years – run a bath, change of underwear, socks, clean T-shirt, brushed his teeth, shaved.

Fuck knows the last time he had bought a new razor.

Saying to Toyah, 'Cut myself shaving.'

Pulling off the Rizla paper.

Toyah saying, 'Now, it's bleeding, again... here, use this.'

Handing Charlie a handkerchief.

Saying, 'It's getting all down your T-shirt.'

Then: 'Is Bobby-Boy seeing somebody?'

The handkerchief smelling of perfume.

Musky.

Charlie saying, 'Seeing somebody?'

'Some tart.'

Charlie offering back the handkerchief.

Covered in blood.

Toyah saying, 'You keep it, Charlie.'

Charlie saying, 'You should be asking Bobby-Boy… not me.'

'You're his batman. You should know.'

Charlie saying, 'I'm the last to know anything.'

Toyah, then, saying, 'How come you don't follow me around like you used to?'

Charlie, pocketing the handkerchief, saying, 'I wouldn't want to get on the wrong side of Winston.'

'But, you don't mind getting on the wrong side of Bobby-Boy?'

'I never said that.'

Toyah saying, 'Anyway, me and Winston… we're not an item any more.'

'Why are you telling me this?'

'I'm grateful, Charlie. You know how to keep your mouth shut.'

Then: 'I have two suitcases packed and ready to go.'

'Go where?'

'That's the problem.'

Then: 'That stuff, before… about suicide? You're not thinking of topping yourself, are you?'

Charlie laughing.

Saying, 'Toyah, my life is so pointless, what would be the point?'

Toyah thinking, Hidden depths?

Or, what?

7

Boxey Carter and Dennis The Diceman were like that… went back so far they used words like 'jankers', 'sprog' and 'mufti', phrases like 'demob happy' and 'stand by your beds', fell about laughing when one of them said, 'If it doesn't move, paint it white,' the rest of the world no idea what the fuck they were on about. Met up when they were both LACs – Leading Aircraftsmen – stationed at RAF Tangmere, in West Sussex.

Doing their National Service.

That far back.

Dennis had first introduced Boxey to the lads when Club 67

was Red Sonja's – 'salad days', according to Dennis – Beryl still fuelling adult male fantasies with her mane of wild red hair and the Amazonian leather gear, Boxey, never slow in coming forward, explaining to Beryl, everybody else listening, how he had come to be called Boxey, saying it was on account of his habit, when ripping off domestic electrical goods, to check out the attic, basement, junk room, garage, garden shed… nine times out of ten he would find the original boxes and polystyrene packaging – those little bags of granules that soaked up the damp, even – the owners storing the boxes in case they ever needed to take the goods back – then, forgetting about them. Boxey Carter saying, 'Full PC set-up, Currys or Dixons – keyboard, monitor, modem, scanner, printer – how much would that set you back, eighteen hundred? No boxes, knocked off gear, you or I would expect to clear three, maybe, four hundred. *In* the boxes, we are talking anything up to a grand.'

Charlie Paul saying, 'What that means… the box that the goods come in is worth more than the goods in the box.'

The Diceman saying, 'But, only if the goods are in the box.'

Beryl saying, 'I pass.'

Boxey saying to Charlie, 'You're not so daft.'

Bobby-Boy saying, 'Don't you believe it.'

Bobby-Boy, now, surprised to see Boxey at the bar with Dennis, knew he had been in the West Middlesex, bypass surgery, saying to Boxey, 'How's the ticker?'

Boxey Carter…

Five foot nothing… wide as he was tall.

Laurel to The Diceman's Hardy.

The Diceman, aware of how they looked together, always saying to Boxey, 'Here's another nice mess you've gotten me into.'

Beryl saying, 'Wasn't it "fine"?'

The Diceman saying, 'Fine what?'

'Fine mess.'

Boxey saying, 'No, it was "nice".'

Then: 'Stand by your beds, eh, Dennis?'

Coming to attention.

Both of them laughing.

119

Right double act.

Boxey, now, saying, 'As new.'

Bobby-Boy saying, 'What you say to all the customers.'

Then: 'Good to see you back on your feet.'

'Straight in and out, nowadays, Bobby-Boy.'

'Should have kept up the National Insurance stamps, right?'

Then: 'Afternoon I've had... you wouldn't believe.'

Beryl saying, 'Is that good or bad?'

Dennis saying, 'Does this mean it might be your round?'

'Name your poison.'

Boxey saying, 'Sod's law, right? Bobby-Boy pushes the boat out, and I'm sworn off the booze.'

Beryl saying, 'Must have been some afternoon.'

Boxey saying, 'Fuck it... as we're celebrating. Give me a G&T.'

Dennis saying, '*You* sure about that?'

Boxey saying, 'You're not my mother, Dennis.'

The Diceman, shaking his head, saying, 'Mine's a large scotch.'

Bobby-Boy saying, to Beryl, 'Two of those... and whatever you're having.'

Thinking, Eighteen thousand, seven hundred and twenty-two pounds...

Fives.

Tens.

Twenties.

All used notes.

All mixed.

In carrier bags.

Stuffed in drawers.

Cupboards.

Biscuit tins.

A teapot.

Under cushions.

Under the mattress.

In the airing cupboard.

In black plastic rubbish sacks in the bathroom.

In the freezer compartment of the fridge.

In the cooker.

Could you believe that… in the cooker?

Bobby-Boy raising his glass, saying, 'To Mrs Irene Evangelides… may she rest in peace.'

Got the 'Irene' from her pension book.

Beryl saying, 'You come into some money?'

'In a manner of speaking.'

One of the top drawers, dresser in the old lady's bedroom, the drawer full of small change… Bobby-Boy could hardly get the drawer open. Plenty of pound coins and 50 p pieces. Bobby-Boy wondering if it was worth sifting.

Deciding against.

No idea when the son was due to arrive from New Zealand.

Saying to Beryl, 'Seen Charlie?'

Beryl saying, 'He was in earlier… got a call from your Toyah.'

'Toyah… after Charlie?'

Boxey saying, 'It's always the quiet ones.'

Dennis saying, 'That counts Charlie out.'

Bobby-Boy saying, 'Oh, do fuck off.'

Thinking about the Mickey Mouse doll, green shorts, propped up against the dressing table mirror, deciding to take it as a present for Yvonne, get her to take the night off – maybe, persuade her to give up the table dancing, altogether – go out for a meal, one of those smart French restaurants down the High Road.

Expensive.

But, what the fuck.

Telling Dennis about the Mickey Mouse doll.

Dennis saying, 'You mind if I took a look?'

Bobby-Boy saying, 'An expert opinion would do no harm.'

Going out to the BMW.

Coming back with the doll.

Dennis inspecting the doll, taking it over to the light, saying, 'Steiff, circa 1930, better known for their teddy bears, worth between two and three grand at auction… really is your lucky day, Bobby-Boy.'

Bobby-Boy starting to worry.

121

Always did, when things were going too well.

Deciding, forget the present – the meal would have to do – excusing himself, going to the other end of the bar, calling Yvonne, Robert picking up on the fourth ring.

Robert saying, 'Bobby-Boy... she's in the shower. Shall I get her to call you back?'

Very matter of fact.

Robert and Yvonne both nineteen, Bobby-Boy thirty-six – that old! – Robert not even *seeing* Bobby-Boy as a contender.

Bobby-Boy saying, 'You don't waste any time.'

How could he be angry with Robert?

Eighteen thousand, seven hundred and twenty-two pounds.

Still wondering why he had taken two of the pound coins.

Robert saying, 'This afternoon... how did it go?'

'It went fine. There'll be a twenty in it for you.'

Robert saying, 'I told you... you don't need to bother.'

Bobby-Boy thinking, Fuck-wit.

Going back to the others.

The Diceman saying, 'Hello? Who rattled your drum?'

Then: 'What's the matter, Bobby-Boy?'

Bobby-Boy saying, 'Fuck knows what's the matter... fuck should I know?'

Beryl about to say, Yellow card.

Thinking better of it.

8

David sitting at the top of the first floor landing stairs, for the life of him, couldn't seem to get his legs to make it any further.

Feeling distinctly shaky.

Not seeing clearly.

Helped if he closed one eye... but, not two.

Closing two eyes was a disaster.

Remembering his phone call to Sophie from the pub bar.

Finally, got through to her.

Sophie saying, 'You have the absolute gall to ring here? After what you did?'

Then: 'How dare you!'

David saying, 'Sophie, I don't understand.'

Then: 'Isn't it what you wanted… that we should be together?'

Sophie saying, 'What I wanted?'

Then: '*What I wanted!*'

Saying, 'Do you realise, I'm afraid… no, I *dread* walking down the street, now, in case I should bump in to you?'

David saying, 'Dread? That's a mite heavy, isn't it?'

Sophie saying, 'You pompous fool.'

Imagine, Sophie calling him that…

Pompous fool.

Aware of the figure looking down at him.

Zöe.

The Leon's daughter.

Holding her Teletubby.

Po.

That's what she called it.

Zöe calling out, 'Mummy! Daddy! Wake up. Man sick.'

David getting to his feet.

Christ! How many pints of ESB *did* he have?

Sick?

Throwing up all over Zöe.

chapter eight

'Time! Time!'

1

Bobby-Boy coming downstairs to the kitchen feeling like shit, cursing the sunlight streaming in through the top landing window, needing coffee and paracetamol – fuck knows how much he put away at the club last night – seeing Toyah at the kitchen table counting the money.

Mrs Irene Evangelides's money.

No... *his* money.

Toyah up to eleven thousand, five-hundred.

Saying, 'Good day at the office?'

Then: 'What time did you crawl in last night?'

Bobby-Boy saying, 'Fuck you think you're doing?'

Toyah, looking up, saying, 'Housekeeping.'

Bobby-Boy filling a kettle.

Spooning coffee into the cafetière.

Saying to Toyah, 'That needs banking. You want to come? A couple of days in Guernsey might do us some good.'

'You are joking? The only good thing about Guernsey this time of year is that it's not full of fuck-wits think Guernsey is a great place to be for a summer holiday.'

'We could splash out. How about the Royal Majestic in the old port?'

Then: 'Prince Albert used to stay at the Royal Majestic.'

124

'Prince Albert used to go to Bognor, too. *That* supposed to tempt me?'

Toyah thinking about Winston.

His Prince Albert.

That feeling.

Bobby-Boy saying, 'Suit yourself.'

'I intend to.'

Bobby-Boy pulling the plug on the kettle, avoiding the whistle, last thing he needed, pouring hot water in the cafetière, taking a cup from the overhead cupboard, sugar from another cupboard, milk from the fridge, Toyah saying, 'No, I didn't want a coffee.'

Bobby-Boy saying, 'You want a coffee?'

Toyah saying, 'No, but, thanks for asking.'

Bobby-Boy saying, 'Oh, do fuck off.'

Pouring his coffee.

Then, saying, 'I hear Charlie Paul was sniffing round.'

'Is that a question?'

'What was he after… apart from the obvious?'

'Do me a favour, Bobby-Boy.'

Then: 'We went for a drink.'

'You and Charlie?'

'Is that a problem?'

'You tell me?'

Then: 'The fuck is all this, Toyah?'

Toyah saying, 'I asked him to help me move.'

'Move?'

Then: 'You seen the paracetamol?'

'As in, I'm leaving you.'

'You're thinking of *leaving* me?'

'Did I mention, "thinking"?'

Bobby-Boy saying, 'Where will you go?'

Toyah saying, 'Funny… that's exactly what Charlie said.'

2

Janet, David's ex-wife, saying, 'I'm back. It's what you wanted, isn't it?' Then: 'With Fiona and Melanie out from under our feet it will be like a second honeymoon.' David saying, 'What about

Sophie?' Janet saying, 'Sophie? *That* whore? Will you never learn?' Janet... her long pale body that David had never found attractive. The exaggerated bush of her pubic hair, why did she never think to trim it when she shaved her legs, shaved her armpits? Embracing the angularity of her, nothing soft, nothing giving... nothing loving. Janet saying, 'Look at you when I left, absolutely pathetic. So, don't try telling me you're not pleased.'

Then...

That voice.

The child-like simper.

Hardly bearable in a young girl... in a middle-aged woman, utterly repugnant. Janet saying, 'Does Davy-wavey want to put his big thingy-wingy in little Janet-wanet?' Holding David close, her pubic bush like a toilet brush against his bare abdomen. David remembering, the two of them still living in the first house in Barnes, Janet on her high horse about something or other, David saying, 'Barnes women are like Richmond women except they go to the gym more often.'

Janet saying, 'What's that supposed to mean?'

David saying, 'It means Barnes women try that little bit too hard.'

Janet saying, 'You pompous idiot.'

Then: 'You should hear yourself, sometimes.'

David aware that Janet was doing it now.

Trying that little bit too hard.

Pressing against him, saying, 'See? See how much you want it.'

Then: 'Some things, a man can't lie about.'

David trying to remember the last time he had made love to Janet – how many years ago? Remembering only, when he was coming, Janet saying, 'Do you *have* to shout in my ear?'

Shaking his shoulders.

Saying, 'You want me! You *do* want me!'

David's bladder about to burst.

His prick, ramrod stiff.

Why should that always be...?

Peter Leon saying, 'Wake up, David! It's seven o'clock. I want you up and out of this house.'

126

Then: 'I mean, now!'

Head pounding.

Everything Sophie's fault.

If she hadn't been so bloody heartless… led him on, then backing off.

Teasing.

Playing with him.

Bloody woman.

Karen Leon, standing in the bedroom door, arms folded, saying, 'Don't look at me. If it had been up to me you would have been out last night.'

Seeing the erection bulging David's underpants.

Saying, 'Oh, charming.'

Peter Leon saying, 'For God's sake!'

Karen saying, 'Five minutes, Peter. I want him out of here.'

David saying, 'I have to use the toilet.'

Coming back to him…

Zöe.

The vomit.

Karen saying, 'I'm not joking.'

David saying, 'Must have been something I ate.'

Then: 'I'm so terribly sorry.'

Peter saying, 'It's too late for sorry.'

Karen saying, 'Amen to that.'

David saying, 'A little privacy, perhaps?'

Thinking of Zöe.

The expression on her face.

Peter and Karen Leon shocked when he started laughing.

Couldn't help himself.

3

'You think, because I have tattoos, wear body jewellery, I should live in a tip?'

'That isn't what I said.'

'It's what you implied.'

Winston's ground floor flat, Carrington Road, North Sheen, fives minutes from the Gloucester House Gate to Richmond Park,

Winston jogging five miles most mornings, learnt to hate dogs, some dog walker, distant voice calling to her animal, just before Fido arrived intent on ripping through flesh and bone... every fucking time. The flat – bought with money his Aunt Anastasia left him – a combined living room and bedroom, futon rolled up against one wall, kitchenette beyond a pine shelved divider, extractor above the gas cooker. The walls all painted white with pale grey wood trim and door, light fixtures chrome silver, rush mat flooring, no television, no books, newspapers, magazines... no mess.

Aluminium framed album cover on the wall.

Never Mind the Bollocks.

Nothing else.

Winston saying, 'You learn to live without it.'

Sophie saying, 'Without what?'

'The bollocks.'

Wondering if he should tell Sophie about the dog this morning – would she scold him like an angry mother? – brown cocker spaniel, Winston scooping up the dog without breaking stride, closing its jaws with one hand, the other gripping its ruff, swinging the dog on its own weight, the way you would a chicken, breaking its neck.

Tossing the dead animal into the undergrowth.

Hearing the owner calling, 'Caliban!'

Saying, now, to Sophie, 'Would you call a dog Caliban?'

Sophie saying, 'Caliban was a Shakespearian villain... The Tempest. I suppose it would depend on the nature of the dog.'

Winston saying, 'Aren't all dogs the same?'

Then: 'A fucking nuisance?'

Sophie saying, then, about the flat, 'It's so spartan... without clutter. The room of an aesthete.'

'Aesthete?'

'Someone who appreciates simplicity... like a monk.'

Winston saying, 'Are you always this patronising?'

'I didn't mean—'

'You mean ascetic.'

'Oh... do I?'

Sophie wearing a navy brushed jersey blouse, the blouse hanging loose over dark chinos, charcoal Mary Jane's with wedge heels. Going for the sophisticated older woman look…

The actress, Francesca Annis.

Attractive, but not necessarily available.

Who did she think she was kidding?

Winston reaching forward.

One hand undoing the smoked pearl buttons of her blouse, starting from the bottom. Sophie saying, 'What are you doing?'

Winston saying, 'Take it off.'

Exposing the grey lace bra.

Winston saying, 'And that.'

'I'm self-conscious.'

'You're beautiful.'

Winston dropping to his knees.

Pulling down the chinos.

The matching grey lace panties.

4

Bobby-Boy reversing out of the parking slot, back of Charlie Paul's block, Addison Gardens, right hand pouring blood despite he had one of Charlie's T-shirts wrapped around it, thinking, One of Charlie's T-shirts? Recipe for gangrene, or what? Worried about getting blood all over the interior, not looking where he was going, too pissed off to concentrate on his driving, backing – smack! – into the milk float. Bobby-Boy thinking, Milk float, for fuck's sake? How many milk floats are there left in London, and I have to back into one of them?

Saying to the milkman, mid-forties, picture of health, sleeves rolled up tight around his biceps – macho man, didn't feel the cold: 'Fuck did you come from?'

Checking out the damage.

Saying, 'This, I do not believe.'

Rear off-side wing caved in, indicator and rear light gone, Bobby-Boy looking at a new panel and spray job, could see the mechanic, now, sharp intake of breath, knowing shake of the head, saying, 'It will cost.'

The milkman, all the time in the world, checking the float, the rear platform where the milk crates were stacked, the angular metal corner responsible for the grief to Bobby-Boy's motor, Bobby Boy saying, 'The most exciting thing happened to you all year, right?'

The milkman saying, 'You want to get that looked at.'

Bobby Boy's hand... dripping blood on to the pavement.

Then: 'I'll need your particulars.'

Bobby-Boy saying, 'The fuck for? Show me one fucking scratch.'

The milkman saying, 'Nasty knock... could be all kinds of problems surface later.'

Then: 'Where there's personal injury involved, the police have to be informed.'

Bobby Boy thinking, All I fucking need.

Not bothering to explain.

Handing the milkman two twenties.

Saying, 'Go away.'

Fifteen minutes earlier, on Charlie Paul's front balcony, Charlie standing in the door in vest and underpants, Bobby-Boy still hungover, each Marlboro Light tasting worse than the one before, thinking, Fuck knows how many nights in a row Charlie had slept in those underpants, didn't bear contemplating, palming Charlie – hard – on the shoulder.

Then again.

And again.

Each shove harder than the last.

Saying, 'Fuck you think you're playing at, Charlie?'

Then: 'I ought to bust your fucking face!'

Charlie saying, 'I don't need this, Bobby-Boy.'

Bobby-Boy saying, 'You think I'm fucking blind?'

Then: 'You think I don't know you've been trying to get into Toyah's knickers for fucking years?'

Then: 'Jesus fucking shit!'

Shoving Charlie again.

Charlie saying, 'She called me... what was I supposed to do? Tell her to fuck off?'

To the left of the front door, four panelled window with frosted glass, toilet off the front hall. When he was a kid, Bobby-Boy used to stand on the balcony wall in these flats, blow raspberries down the overflow pipe, the noise reverberating in the toilet cistern, scare the shit out of whoever was sitting in there…

Bobby-Boy saying, 'Why me, God? What the fuck have I done to deserve this?'

Then: 'Fucking bollocks!'

Punching his fist through the bottom right hand frosted glass panel.

Saying, 'Oh, shit!'

Charlie, looking at Bobby-Boy's hand, blood everywhere, glass shards poking out of the flesh, saying, 'That looks nasty… I better run you up the hospital.'

Bobby-Boy saying, 'Go fuck yourself.'

The milkman, now, not taking the two twenties.

Saying, 'Cuts no ice with me, you waving money around.'

Bobby-Boy saying, 'Then, you can go fuck yourself, too.'

The milkman needing to think about that.

Saying, 'Too?'

5

Yvonne and Robert in bed, *Ready Steady Cook* just started on the television, Fern Britton introducing today's guest cooks, Robert saying, 'You watch this?'

Yvonne saying, 'My version of breakfast television.'

'You like cooking?'

'I *never* cook.'

'Pity… I was feeling peckish.'

Yvonne saying, 'You must be confusing me with your mother.'

On the television, now, one of the guest cooks; big, shambling man with ginger-blond hair and a beard, Robert saying, 'Looks like a German,' then: 'You find a hair in your soup, no prizes where it came from.'

Yvonne saying, 'They don't often cook soup… it's all in the presentation at the end. Soup never picks up many votes.'

Explaining the way it worked.

How two members of the audience had each been invited to bring along five pounds' worth of basic ingredients from which each of the two guest cooks was expected to produce a mouth-watering meal in only twenty minutes, the live audience then voting for which of the two cooks had prepared the most exciting dishes from the ingredients provided...

Green peppers to the right.

Red tomatoes to the left.

Robert saying, 'You are sad... you know that?'

The first participant now dumping out his carrier bag of provisions – an aubergine, two large tomatoes, a packet of mozzarella cheese, spaghetti, one onion, a quarter of sliced ham off the bone. Fern Britton, the presenter saying, 'And this cost you how much?'

Yvonne saying, 'Nil out of ten for originality.'

Then: 'Did you know, there used to be a pop programme, early Friday night, called *Ready Steady Go*... the weekend starts here. Bobby-Boy was telling me about it.'

Robert saying, 'I should be at work.'

Yvonne saying, 'Would you sooner be?'

'I need the money.'

Then: 'You've got to be kidding.'

Yvonne saying, 'I'm going to have to throw you out at seven. Get myself together. I need to be out of the house by eight.'

'Would you miss work for me?'

'No way.'

Robert saying, 'I don't like it... what you do for a living.'

Yvonne saying, 'Which is what they all say five minutes before I dump them.'

'Did Bobby-Boy say that?'

'He didn't get that far.'

On the television, the two cooks explaining what they intended to do with the ingredients... the spaghetti was to become a pasta *fritata* topped with tomato sauce, the aubergines sliced lengthwise and fried in olive oil, topped with ham and mozzarella cheese, finished in the oven...

132

The other cook was going to make a tower.

Sweet potato mash.

Calves liver.

Lamb's lettuce…

Robert saying, 'A tower?'

Yvonne saying, 'Arty-tarty.'

Then: 'Bet it wins.'

Robert saying, 'You think he will be pissed off with me… Bobby-Boy?'

'Why should Bobby-Boy be pissed off with you?'

'This.'

Then: 'Us.'

Yvonne saying, '"This" is nothing to do with him. As for the "us", well, don't go jumping the gun.'

Then: 'Are you afraid of him?'

'Afraid of Bobby-Boy? Why should I be afraid of Bobby-Boy?'

'The way you are of this Winston character.'

'You would have to be stupid, not to be afraid of Winston Capaldi.'

Then: 'It's difficult to explain.'

'Try.'

'You always feel you want to please Bobby-Boy.'

Then: 'Like he was an older brother.'

Then: 'It's important that he likes you.'

Yvonne saying, 'Bobby-Boy should take a long hard look in the mirror.'

'What are you saying?'

'He's no spring chicken.'

'He's not that old.'

'He is when he's trying to get in your knickers.'

Robert saying, 'What about the weatherman?'

Then: 'She dresses like she should be reading the weather forecast.'

Fern Britton.

Two-piece blue suit.

Yvonne saying, 'Wrong colour.'

Then: 'You know about the weatherman?'

133

Then: 'Let's just say I didn't fancy doing two geriatrics in a row.'

Not comfortable.

Moving on…

Saying, 'Did you know… the average male reaches orgasm in under five minutes?'

And: 'Also, one in twenty men never have sex.'

And: 'One in seven men experiences difficulty in achieving an erection.'

Then: 'Thank Christ, I'm a woman.'

Robert saying, 'How come you know all this?'

'*She* magazine… there was a copy in the doctor's waiting room.'

'What were you doing at the doctor's?'

'Girl trouble.'

'Girl trouble? What's girl trouble?'

'What you're not meant to ask about, dummy.'

Robert saying, 'Is it true… those tampon ads on the telly?'

'What about them?'

'That women's period blood is blue… not red?'

Yvonne saying, 'You've got to be joking!'

Seeing Robert's face…

Saying, 'Bastard!'

Robert saying, 'You need to be careful.'

Then: 'That word can get you into deep shit.'

Then: 'I'm offended. You actually believed I could think that?'

Yvonne saying, 'The article also said that the average white Caucasian penis is six inches long… they got this from a condom manufacturer's survey.'

'What am I supposed to say?'

'Nothing… just be grateful.'

Then: 'It's the "orgasm in under five minutes" that needs working on.'

'What can we do about it?'

'We? It's more a matter of what can *you* do about it.'

'Like what?'

'Like try thinking about something else while you're doing it.'

134

'Like what?'

'Like – for example – Winston Capaldi.'

Robert saying, 'Winston Capaldi?'

Then: 'You want me to be one of the one in seven?'

'I don't get you?'

Robert saying, 'Think about it.'

On the television, Fern Britton saying, 'OK, you have twenty minutes starting from… NOW!'

Yvonne saying, 'You hear that?'

Later…

Fern Britton saying, 'One minute left.'

Background music going into overdrive.

Yvonne saying, 'Ignore the bitch.'

6

Turnham Green.

Bench facing the High Road.

The man saying, 'Kos.'

'What?'

'Island in the Dodecanese… twenty-one across.'

David filling in the word in his *Guardian* Quick Crossword.

Saying, 'Actually, I would have got that.'

The man saying, 'With a "K", not a "C". Otherwise you'll never get six down… "Die".'

Then: 'Kick the bucket.'

David saying, 'I don't wish to appear rude, but, don't you have your own crossword to do?'

'Do mine at breakfast… over a cup of tea.'

Then: 'What you like with the main one… the cryptic?'

'Hopeless. I see the answers, I still can't work out *why* they are the answers.'

'It's a knack. You get used to the way they operate.'

Then: 'You can blame the supermarkets.'

'You've lost me.'

'Kos… spelt with a "C". The lettuces.'

Then: 'You a drinking man?'

'Why on earth should you say that?'

'You're sitting on a park bench since ten o'clock waiting for the pub to open?'

'That's a huge presumption.'

'But, a correct one, am I right?'

The man holding out his hand, saying, 'Charles.'

Then: 'I'm an actor... resting at the moment.'

David saying, 'Would I have seen you in anything?'

Charles saying, 'MFI ad a little while ago.'

Then: 'Hey-up... they're opening.'

David, no option but to walk with Charles.

Entering the pub – The Old Packhorse – Charles saying to the barman, 'A pint of your finest ale, my good man.'

David thinking, Oh, my God!

The bore to end all bores.

Grateful that Charles had not offered to buy him a drink.

Charles saying, 'None of that, "Speed of the slowest ship", right?'

David saying, 'Couldn't agree more.'

No idea what Charles was talking about.

Charles saying... how many hours later? The lunchtime crowd been and gone. One or two groups of businessmen still earnestly discussing whatever it was they had to discuss in order to make a living, a visiting sales rep buying all the drinks, asking at the bar for a receipt for the Thai lunches. A couple holding hands across a table, gazing into each other's eyes, the man appreciably older than the woman – David thinking, Office romance...? Reminded of that brief period at the start of their affair, he and Sophie, some remote bar, unable *not* to touch, afraid that a friend or acquaintance would happen upon them... perhaps, willing it to happen – isolated drinkers, in for the duration, Zen Buddhists contemplating their glasses, two women, power dressers, both using mobiles at regular intervals, one saying to a man in his seventies, casual grey suit with a thin red check, yellow cravat, brown suede shoes, flat cap, immaculate bushy grey moustache, mid-day edition of the *Evening Standard* turned to the racing pages, 'Do you mind... your smoke...' The man pointing his cigarette, holding it as if it where a fencing foil, saying, 'My dear lady, if you require a smoke-free zone, might I suggest a London Transport bus?'

Old Ted.

Everybody knew Old Ted.

The last of the sports.

Charles saying...

'Oldest pub in Chiswick. Been a pub on this site since the seventeen hundreds. It was the first staging post out of London heading west along the Bath Road.' And: 'When the old Chiswick Empire still existed, there used to be a tunnel from back-stage to this bar... it's why they still have a theatrical theme, all these music hall posters on the walls.' And: 'Turnham Green, across the road, was the site of the last decisive battle of the Civil War... where Cromwell's men halted the Royalist march on London.'

David saying, 'My wife... my ex-wife. Did I tell you?'

Charles saying, 'When the old Chiswick Empire closed down, do you know who it was they asked to do the very last show... came all the way over from Las Vegas to do it?'

David saying, 'Abso-bloody-lutely no idea – my ex-wife, that is... do you know, our Fiona was going out with this chap, Toby. All the youngsters were wearing those baggy T-shirts, baggy jeans with the crutch down around their knees, pretending they were black. Could hardly understand one word any of them were saying... left out all the definite and indefinite articles, in fact, most of the time, all they retained was verb and object.'

'Liberace.'

Then: 'Happy to do it, he was, too. Said the Chiswick Empire was his all-time favourite venue.'

'So, Toby says, "Goin' pictures, innit, Mrs Cornish." The "innit" they added to everything, right? It wasn't *meant* to make any sense. My wife, stupid cow, says to Toby, "Isn't it? dear, not *innit*".'

'Saw Old Mother Riley at the Empire when I was a kid... and Lonnie Donegan. He was in Christmas pantomime, Aladdin.'

'Missed the point, entirely.'

Charles saying, 'Talking of crosswords.'

David thinking, *Were* we talking of crosswords?

137

Charles saying, 'Drachm.'

'What?'

'Drachm... one of the answers last week. Completely threw me. You know what a drachm is?'

'*Guardian* misprint? Drachma without the "a"?'

'An eighth of a fluid ounce.'

Then: 'You know that?'

David saying, 'Time for a refill.'

Charles placing his hand over David's, stroking David's hand, saying, 'Look, if you need a place to stay?'

David saying, 'That's very kind.'

Then: 'But, I think not.'

7

The futon – unrolled – converting the living room into a bedroom... hessian blinds in the bay window pulled against the low afternoon sunlight, Sophie saying, 'Why didn't you... you know, last time?'

Winston saying, 'You were out of it.'

Then: 'I don't take advantage.'

Sophie saying, 'I wouldn't have minded.'

Winston saying, '"Wouldn't have minded" isn't enough.'

'You knew, though?'

'I knew.'

Sophie saying, 'Do men always know?'

'Unless they're thick.'

Sophie biting down on the ring that pierced Winston's right nipple – horse champing at the bit – her other hand between his legs, little finger, the only finger that would fit, squeezing through the ring that impaled his prick... earlier, Winston, his hand between *her* legs, daubing Sophie's body with their juices, drawing circles on her stomach, around her nipples, Sophie saying, 'Don't you have *any* shame?'

Winston saying, 'You like it.'

Then: 'Don't you?'

Sophie saying, 'Fish and finger pie.'

'What?'

138

'"Strawberry Fields Forever".'

Then: 'The Beatles.'

Then: 'No – tell a lie – the other side, "Penny Lane".'

Singing: 'Let me take you down.'

Saying, 'I always preferred "Strawberry Fields"… John Lennon.'

Winston saying, 'They had *that* in a song? Fish and finger pie?'

'Nobody knew what it meant.'

'From what I've heard—'

'Wildly over-rated.'

'What?'

'The Swinging '60s… we were all such innocents.'

Winston saying, 'Tell me about the boy.'

'What boy?'

'Your boy.'

Then: 'Your child of the '60s.'

Sophie saying, 'You know about my son?'

Then: 'Aurelie, she told you, didn't she?'

Then: 'I don't want to talk about it.'

'Why… do you feel guilty?'

'Why should I feel guilty?'

'Abandoning him.'

Sophie saying, 'Perhaps, I had better go.'

Winston saying, 'Earlier, you were asking… the age thing?'

Then: 'Your finger is trapped.'

Grinning, saying, 'That answer your question?'

'You're not funny.'

Then: 'Don't!'

'How else will you release it?'

Sophie groaning.

Thinking, *Wicked! Wicked! Wicked!*

Winston, still grinning, thinking, What goes around comes around.

chapter nine

'Couldn't be arsed!'

1

Toyah saying, 'Two thousand, Charlie. That suit you?'

Charlie saying, 'I want no part of it.'

'You're joking me?'

'This is between you and Bobby-Boy.'

Then: 'It's not what I had in mind, Toyah. All I did was give you a call, tell you Bobby-Boy was on his way to the hospital, might need some help.'

Toyah saying, 'Yeah, well, one thing leads to another, right?'

Lazio's Coffee Bar and Continental Patisserie, main intersection, Hammersmith Broadway Shopping Precinct, opposite the Tesco Mini-Mart, office workers buying something from the chilled shelf to take home, microwave for supper, a busker working the pedestrian subway to Fulham Palace Road, playing, 'The Drugs Don't Work,' *Big Issue* vendor calling out, '*Big Issue*... help the homeless.' Across the intersection, beyond the flower seller and the moving stairway up to the bus station, the underground entrance, long queue at the automatic ticket dispenser, tourist at the ticket counter waving a map... Lazio's all etched glass and chrome, high stools, daily newspapers for the clientele to read, Charlie Paul, no idea what to order, saying, 'White coffee?' Toyah, checking the list, saying, 'Make that two Blue

Mountain *lattes*, cinnamon top.' Saying to Charlie, 'What you ordered, only, with the cinnamon.'

Charlie saying, 'Will I like cinnamon?'

Toyah saying, 'Suck it and see.'

Charlie thinking, *One thing leads to another*.

Saying, 'Chance would be a fine thing.'

Toyah saying, 'Just don't, OK?'

Charlie's yellow Volkswagen Polo parked in the Apollo theatre car park, underneath Hammersmith Flyover, Charlie worried that Bobby-Boy will spot the motor coming round Hammersmith Broadway, Toyah saying, 'Relax, Charlie, enjoy your coffee.'

Brown Gladstone bag between her feet.

Under the table.

Saying, 'You're a good friend, Charlie, but, that's as far as it goes.'

Then: 'As far as it will ever go.'

Charlie saying, 'What will you do? Now you have the money?'

'Do? I'm going to go home, watch Bobby-Boy sweat.'

Charlie saying, 'You know, it's funny, Toyah... I don't think I would ever cheat on Bobby-Boy, despite what he thinks.'

Toyah saying, 'Yeah, well... we're never going to find out about that, are we?'

2

Sophie at the kitchen sink washing up her breakfast things, cereal bowl, coffee mug, plate for toast. Through the kitchen window, the back garden a patchwork quilt of fallen leaves, the last splash of colour, a Begonia in a terracotta pot, finally succumbed to the cold, its vivid red blossom faded to brown... Sophie wondering if she should take a hot drink up to Aurelie, encourage her to be out of bed before noon, saying to her, last night, 'But, you must do something with your life.' And, 'You can't sit around the house, half-dressed, watching mindless television *all* the time.'

Meaning, 'My house.'

Not, 'The house.'

Aurelie saying, 'I don't see why not.'

141

Then: 'Winston… he didn't ring, did he?'

Too quickly…

Sophie saying, 'Aurelie, you haven't been out of the house.'

Remembering Jim, when the wheelchair arrived, home care nurse showing them how to open it, adjust the foot-rests, Jim saying, 'If you think I'm going out in that!' Sophie saying, 'Jim, this isn't a time to be proud.' Jim saying, 'Sometimes, "proud" is all you've got.' Picturing him, now, in the wheelchair, beside the sink, holding a dish-cloth, Sophie saying, 'But, we never dry up… we're not a drying up family' – the dishes always left stacked on the draining board till they were next needed – and, 'Anyway, since when did you ever take an active interest in the washing up?'

Jim saying, 'Since I wasn't able to reach the sink.'

'That doesn't make any sense.'

'Think about it.'

Then, Jim saying, 'You know… after I'm gone.'

Sophie saying, 'Don't talk like that.'

'No! Listen! You're a good looking woman, Sophie. Don't waste it.'

'Waste it?'

'You know what I mean.'

'What *do* you mean?'

'Nobody mourns for ever.'

Then: 'There *will* be somebody else. Don't feel bad about it. Let it happen.'

Then: 'Just make sure it's not some fucking creep.'

Some fucking creep.

Like David?

Sophie wondering what Jim would have made of Winston…

Feeling the delicious soreness between her legs.

Her nipples, delicate to the touch.

Wearing a cotton T-shirt – Grey Marl – deck chinos, no bra.

Her feet bare.

Trying to remember the last time she had felt this way.

This good.

Laughing… thinking, Is this what they meant?

A right seeing to?

Thinking, Oh, Jim, I don't feel guilty.

I don't feel guilty, at all.

Watching a grey squirrel raiding the bird-feed that was hanging from the branches of the buddleia... Jim, always, saying, 'Rats with bushy tails. I just don't get it. I really don't.'

Sophie *wanting* to feel guilty.

But, couldn't.

Not even about Aurelie.

Winston, yesterday, saying, 'What will you tell your daughter?'

Sophie saying, 'Suddenly, she's "my daughter".'

'You didn't answer my question.'

'What could I possibly say?'

'The truth?'

Sophie saying, 'Oh, God... it's a mess, isn't it?'

'If you could turn back the clock?'

Sophie...

Thinking of Jim.

Saying, 'That would depend how far.'

3.

Winston with another of those drivers, deciding he was going to have to change his cab company... his mobile ringing, cab driver saying, 'Who do they think they are, right?' Talking about the French – fuck did Winston care about the French? 'They expect us to change the name of *our* station... say it reminds them of the last time we whipped their arses?' Waterloo Station. 'Fucking good job, too. Bit of reminding do no harm at all, you ask me.'

Winston seeing the NO SMOKING sticker.

Times like this, he wished he smoked.

Reaching into the pocket of his bomber jacket.

Cab driver saying, 'Did you see in the paper? One in four Frenchmen doesn't bother to wash his hands after taking a crap.'

Then: 'Filthy bastards!'

Winston pressing YES on the Ericsson.

Coming down off the elevated section into the Marylebone Road, driver indicating a left into Lisson Grove, cutting back

143

towards Paddington, too busy shooting off his mouth, missed the Paddington exit on the overpass. Winston, now, saying, 'One more word.'

Cab driver saying, 'One more word, what?'

Aurelie on the Ericsson.

Saying, 'Hello, stranger.'

Winston saying, 'Is this important?'

Then, to the cab driver, 'Shut the fuck up, would you?'

Aurelie saying, 'You talking to me?'

'That's what you want to think.'

Cab driver, catching Winston's eye in the mirror, saying, 'No call for that.'

Winston saying, 'No?'

Then: 'Try sitting where I'm sitting.'

Aurelie saying, 'Winston, this is boring.'

Cab driver saying, 'Bit of old fashioned civility never did go amiss.'

Winston saying, to Aurelie, 'This is not a good time.'

'You're avoiding me.'

'I've been busy.'

'Yeah? Who with?'

Winston thinking, Ask your mother.

Our mother.

Saying, again, 'Is this important?'

'That would depend on your priorities.'

'What do you want me to say?'

Aurelie surprising Winston.

Saying, 'How's the guitar going?'

Winston, just now, thinking about Eric Holtz... all the kinds of shit he was going to give him, saying, 'The guitar?'

'My dad's guitar... what are you on, Winston?'

'If only.'

Then, getting it.

Aurelie's mistake.

Saying, 'I don't play guitar.'

Seeing the cyclist between the cab and the gutter, coming past on the inside, cab driver about to make another left, road along-

144

side the Seashell fish restaurant, hearing the cyclist bang twice on the roof of the cab before going down.

Cab driver saying, 'Fuck was that?'

Winston saying, 'You ran down a cyclist.'

Cab driver saying, 'Cyclist?'

Then: 'Shouldn't be on the fucking road.'

4

Sophie deciding she would make a leek and potato soup, easy and quick, ingredients to hand, recipe she had picked up from a children's television programme – *Blue Peter* – God knows how long ago… chopping the leeks, big chunks, scraping and chopping the carrots, sweating the leeks and the carrots in butter, peeling the potatoes. Aurelie sitting at the kitchen table, baby-blue knitted top, panties, white fluffy mules, reading a copy of *Hello*, listening to Radio 1, flicking cigarette ash into her cupped hand. Sophie, from the sink, saying, 'If I have to listen to that Celine Dion song one more time I shall scream.'

Aurelie saying, 'Better than your Radio 4.'

Then: '*Woman's Hour*.'

Then: 'There's only so much you need to know about Fallopian tubes.'

Sophie saying, 'What would you know about *Woman's Hour*? It's on in the morning. You're never up in the morning.'

Aurelie saying, 'It didn't used to be.'

Then: 'How long?'

'How long, what?'

'Food.'

Chopped potato into the Le Creuset, enough hot water to cover, vegetable stock cube, fresh parsley, seasoning, Sophie placing the lid on the cooking pot, adjusting the heat, saying, 'When it's ready.'

Then: 'Because you are back living at home, that is no reason to revert to your childhood. You're a grown woman. A divorced woman… it's time you thought about doing something with your life.'

'Spare me.'

Then: 'Pity.'

'Pity, what?'

Aurelie saying, 'Pity that regular sex doesn't seem to have improved your disposition, any.'

'What on earth are you on about?'

Aurelie saying, 'So, where were you all day yesterday? Two hours in front of the mirror trying not to look like you made any effort. Opium behind the ears and God knows where else… don't tell me all that was for the benefit of the check-out operator at Sainsbury's.'

Then: 'Not with that dip-shit, David, I hope?'

'I don't see that it is any of your business who I was with… not that I *was* with anybody.'

'Put it this way… if that low-life is shaping up to be step-daddy, I'm out of here.'

Sophie saying, 'Tempting, but, the price is too high.'

'And, I just thought you were playing hard to get.'

'A little late for that.'

Sophie asleep.

Jim – no, David! – entering her from behind.

David saying, 'How can anything that feels this good not be right?'

Aurelie saying, 'Mum?'

Sophie thinking, Did that make it right?

Her and Winston?

Aurelie saying, 'Come in, number seven.'

Going to the sink, dousing her cigarette under the running tap, throwing it in the waste-bin. Lifting the *Le Creuset* lid, sniffing, saying, 'What is it, anyway?'

'Soup.'

'Soup… is that it?'

Sophie remembering Jim saying, Aurelie still a child, in one of her precocious moods, 'We screwed up, Sophie. Should have ditched the daughter, kept the son.'

Sophie shocked.

Saying, 'How could you joke about such a thing?'

Saying, now, to Aurelie, 'You don't have to eat it.'

Celine Dion back on the radio – different DJ – singing, 'And I will always love you.' Sophie, read somewhere that she was French-Canadian… remembering Jim, back from his only tour of Canada, saying, 'Slough with mountains.'

Aurelie saying, 'You need to lighten up.'

'Lighten up?'

'Go out… have some fun.'

Sophie, her finger still trapped, moving inside herself, moving to Winston's rhythm, Winston saying, 'How often?'

'How often, what?'

'Your hand?'

Sophie saying, 'One minute I'm having a passionate affair, next, I need to lighten up, go out more… I wish you would make up your mind.'

Winston saying, 'Down there.'

Sophie saying, 'Don't! I don't like it!'

Winston saying, 'Yes you do.'

Sophie's body, a traitor to her declarations.

Aurelie saying, 'How about a make-over? You're still an attractive woman… you just need dragging into the twenty-first century.'

'Do you realise how patronising you sound?'

'It's a make-over society we live in, mother. Rooms, gardens, bodies… nothing is ever the same for more than five minutes.'

Sophie coming.

Wave after wave…

Saying to Aurelie, 'In the '60s we thought the *I Ching* was the source of all wisdom.'

… after wave.

'The *I Ching*?'

'*The Chinese Book of Changes*.'

Then: 'You're right. Nobody takes the time to appreciate what they already have any more.'

Checking the soup.

Adding cream. Nutmeg.

Sophie saying, 'We used to think change was for the better, that the alternative was stagnation… now, I'm not so sure.'

Winston saying, 'Now, you do it.'

'Do it?'

'On your own.'

Sophie putting out bread, bowls, spoons, finding the ladle in a drawer, saying to Aurelie, 'You want some of this soup, or not?'

Realising she could come...

Just thinking about it.

5

The nurse saying, 'Slight prick.'

Tetanus injection.

Bobby-Boy thinking, No 'slight' about it... fucked his hand, fucked the motor, Yvonne taking the piss, Charlie taking the piss, Winston ripping him off, Toyah going on about leaving.

Thank Christ for the money.

Eighteen thousand, seven hundred and twenty pounds.

Two for luck.

Gladstone bag...

Boot of the BMW.

Rolling over.

Pulling up his jeans.

The nurse saying, 'There, that wasn't too bad, was it?'

'Just as long as I don't see the needle.'

The nurse, pulling open the cubicle curtains, saying, 'You'd be surprised how many people say that.'

Bobby-Boy's hand stitched, bandaged, X-rayed... nothing broken, the house doctor on call in Accident and Emergency giving Bobby-Boy a hard time, young Indian doctor, Australian accent, Doctor Sikora saying, 'We have our resources stretched far enough without having to minister to fools who bring it upon themselves.' Assuming Bobby-Boy had been in a fight. Bobby-Boy wondering how he could explain, punching his fist through a frosted glass window...

Not doing Charlie.

Doctor Sikora in his mid-twenties.

Bobby-Boy saying, 'Biggest break-through in medicine this century.'

'I'm sorry?'

'Polite doctors... that particular advance must have passed you by.'

Five hours...

Two of those waiting in the X-Ray Department.

Reading old copies of *Cosmopolitan, Hello, The Field, Town and Country, National Geographic*... trying to make sense of one of the notices: *CT SCAN APPOINTMENTS: Would all patients with an 8.10am appointment for a CT Scan please arrive at 8.10am. All patients with an appointment after 8.10am should arrive an hour before the time of their appointment.* Bobby-Boy thinking, Some fuck-wit is earning good money coming up with shit like this, saying, to the woman on reception, Afro-Carribean, head buried in her computer screen, 'That make sense to you?'

The receptionist saying, 'Perfect sense.'

Bobby-Boy saying, 'From Anglesey, right?'

'Anglesey?'

'You.'

Then: 'Little island, north-west corner of Wales, on the way to Dublin?'

'I know where it is.'

'Local rag ran a spot the ball competition, left the ball in by mistake... still, only three people wrote in with the right answer.'

The receptionist saying, 'Take a seat, would you... your name will be called.'

Bobby-Boy saying, 'Promises, promises.'

Now... almost dark, approaching the motor, slip-road between the South Wing of the hospital and the highrise nurses' accommodation, beyond the grass verge and the railings, Fulham Palace Road solid with traffic – been that way since they closed Hammersmith Bridge – only two of the five hours on the meter, Bobby-Boy spotting the wheel-clamp from two hundred yards, thinking, Fucking unbelievable! Keep you hanging around all afternoon, *and* they clamp your motor...

Thirty-five quid.

Insult to fucking injury.

Bobby-Boy counting ten.

149

Slowly.

Refusing to let it get to him.

Walking around to the rear of the BMW, seeing, immediately, that the boot was not secure, thinking, Had to be the crunch with the milk float, not noticing it before now, alignment problems, *more* fucking expense... then thinking, Oh fuck!

Swinging open the boot lid.

No Gladstone Bag.

No eighteen thousand, seven hundred and twenty pounds.

No matter how hard he looked.

6

Winston taking Eric Holtz with his whole body-weight, slamming him backwards, forearm under Eric's chin, Eric's body suspended two inches above the carpet, room key in his hand, back pressed against the hotel corridor wall.

Gilt-framed mirrors.

Flock wallpaper.

Maroon and gold.

Winston reminded of the way Indian restaurants used to look before they got tarted up, before it cost an arm and a leg to eat in them, balti this, balti that... saying to Eric, 'You're giving me the run-around, Eric.'

Eric saying, 'The fuck you think you're doing?'

Then: 'I can't fucking breath.'

Winston saying, 'That's the idea.'

Turning Eric round, pushing his face into the flock wallpaper, left hand gripping Eric's hair – what there was of it – right hand making a fist, proscribing a circle low down and to one side of Eric's back, Eric saying, 'My glasses... you're squashing my glasses.' Winston saying, 'I can leave you pissing blood for a week.'

'Oh, fuck off.'

'You want to rethink that?'

Eric saying, 'It was a piece of harmless fun, for fuck's sake.'

'Harmless fun? At my expense?'

'You pissed Bobby-Boy off.'

'About the guitar?'

150

'What else would there be?'

Then: 'You're fucking hurting!'

Winston picturing Toyah, that ridiculous parrot tattooed on her backside, Toyah saying, 'What's the matter, big man? You never hit a woman before?'

This, in Bobby-Boy's bedroom.

In Bobby-Boy's bed.

After fucking Bobby-Boy's wife.

Winston saying, 'I don't get you?'

Toyah saying, 'Psycho analysis is not on the agenda.'

Hearing the hum of the service lift.

Concertina doors crashing open.

Winston locating the CCTV camera.

Waving.

Releasing Eric Holtz... walking towards the hotel security guard, grey uniform, silver buttons, campaign hat, saying, 'Don't even think about it. Whatever they pay you, it isn't enough.'

The hotel security guard saying, 'Hey, I enjoy my work.'

Winston smiling at the stance, saying, 'Evening classes don't cut it, fuck-wit.' Deciding against the wind-pipe... the eyes. Not wanting a fatal blow, or to inflict permanent damage.

The hotel security guard blocking the kick.

Too slow for the *uraken*.

Clenched fist – back-handed – to the side of the temple.

7

Dennis The Diceman at the bar, whisky and water, packet of cheese and onion crisps, reading aloud from the *Sunday Telegraph* – swore he only bought it on a 'know thine enemy' basis – never tired of quoting Marlon Brando in *The Godfather*, Dennis saying, 'That scene in the garden, just before he pegged it...' Bobby-Boy, once, saying, 'Christ! But you do remind me of my old man.' Dennis saying, 'I would assume that to be a compliment,' then, continuing, 'Marlon says to his son, Michael, "Keep your friends close, but your enemies closer." '

Beryl saying, 'So, what about the *Sun*... what's your excuse for reading that shit?'

Dennis saying, 'Ah, but you are not a native islander.'

Boxey saying, 'Stumm, Dennis.'

Dennis saying, 'If it doesn't move—'

Boxey saying, 'Paint it white.'

Beryl saying, 'And?'

'Sports coverage, my dear Sonja… what else?'

Everybody in Club 67 heard it all a million times.

Dennis, now, reading: '*Burglars face loss of driving licence as penalty.*'

Then: '*Persistent criminals will lose their driving licences under radical Government proposal to punish petty offenders.*'

Boxey saying, 'Counts you out… "petty".'

Dennis laughing, saying, 'Charlie, this is for your benefit, are you listening?'

Charlie Paul, too preoccupied with his own problems… running through how it happened, how he got himself into deep shit with Bobby-Boy; ringing Toyah, telling her Bobby-Boy had hurt himself, might need some help, driving her to Charing Cross Hospital, spotting Bobby-Boy's BMW parked up in a Pay & Display bay, noticing Bobby-Boy's boot, saying to Toyah, 'You think he knows that's open?'

Toyah saying, 'Oh, fuck off, Charlie!'

Charlie wondering how come the whole world kept saying that to him… ?

Fuck off, Charlie.

Saying, 'Looks like he had a crunch.'

Thinking, *That's* what he heard this morning, while he was taking a piss.

Right after Bobby-Boy had gone.

Toyah saying, 'You going to stop, or what?'

Charlie pulling over.

Checking the boot.

Holding up the Gladstone Bag, saying, 'You think this should be under lock and key?'

Toyah, coming round the side of the Polo, saying, 'I'll take that.'

Deep shit.

152

None of it Charlie's fault.

Charlie thinking, So, what's new?

Dennis The Diceman saying, 'Are you listening?'

Reading from the newspaper: *One official said that the meas-ure could "really hit criminals where it hurt… quite frankly, the type of punishments that have been handed out are just water off a duck's back."* '

Then: 'And, *quite frankly*, matey, your take on reality is about as useful as what drops out of a duck's arse… golden rule of motoring, right? You're either one hundred per cent legal or one hundred per cent illegal. Anything in between will cause you grief. Charlie, how many driving licences do you currently possess?'

Charlie saying, 'Should I know?'

'Rough guess?'

'Six?'

Then: 'Why, do you need one?'

Boxey saying, 'Christ, you can be thick at times.'

Charlie thinking, Only 'at times'?

Things are looking up.

Dennis The Diceman saying, 'I'm simply making a point… that this New Labour government doesn't know its arse from its elbow. The *real* Labour government sowed the seeds of its own destruction back in the '60s when it opened up the universities to the working classes. Next you know, there's the nouveau middle-classes, red-brick graduates, taking over the party machine, fuck-ing the labour movement for ever… is that ironic, or what?'

Charlie saying, 'You say so, Dennis.'

'I do say so, Charlie.'

Boxey saying, 'Arise, Sir Alf.'

Then: 'Send 'em all back to the gash trades, I say.'

Beryl rolling her eyes.

No idea what 'gash' meant.

Dennis saying, 'Did you see the results of this new think-tank they commissioned on social status… teachers – teachers, I fuck-ing ask you! – come in top, musicians second, royalty are way down the list at number four. You picture, some second grade physics teacher goes into the Ivy, says, "Sorry, but I haven't

153

booked." Major Domo says, "Oh, that won't be a problem, sir. Now, let me see… shall we shunt Prince Edward or Sean Connery?" '

Then: 'In your dreams.'

Beryl saying, 'He's on one.'

'Waiters… eighth, right? Bottom of the list after cleaners, traffic wardens, dustbinmen… so this second grade physics teacher with the leather patches on his elbows and a Biro stain on his top pocket is sitting there, best table in the Ivy, wine waiter can tell him everything there is to know about a nice bottle of Chateau Latour '79, all teach is interested in is whether the Lambrusco is nice and cold.'

Telephone behind the bar ringing.

Charlie saying, 'Saved by the bell.'

Boxey saying, 'I wouldn't mind if he paid taxes.'

Beryl saying, 'It's for you, Charlie… Bobby-Boy.'

'Bobby-Boy? For me?'

Dennis saying, 'Clock his face!'

Beryl saying, 'How come, Charlie, you always have a problem imagining any phone call could be for you?'

Boxey saying, 'Wants to know why his missus was after him, yesterday.'

Dennis saying, 'The plot thickens.'

Boxey saying, 'Stand by your beds!'

Bobby-Boy, on the phone, saying to Charlie, 'I'm up Charing Cross. You got thirty-five quid?'

'Thirty-five quid? '

'I've been clamped.'

Charlie, turning to Dennis, saying, 'Bobby-Boy's short. You got thirty-five quid spare?'

Dennis saying, 'Not last night, he wasn't.'

Peeling off forty – two twenties – from a roll, saying, 'Here, tell him this is on account for the Clarice Cliff.'

'Bobby-Boy?'

'I've gone nowhere, Charlie.'

'I'm on my way.'

Then: 'Bobby-Boy?'

154

'What?'

'This isn't some kind of set-up?'

'Set-up?'

Falling in.

Saying, 'Grow up, Charlie, for fuck's sake.'

chapter ten

'Are we go, now?'

1

David could not believe he was doing this... or, rather, believe he was allowing this to be done to him. Charles's two bedroomed flat, above a pizza takeaway, Goldhawk Road, could see the Metropolitan Line bridge from the bedroom window, entrance to Shepherd's Bush Market on the left, bus garage on the right, double-deckers turning in and out of the garage, holding up traffic, Charles with his head between David's thighs sucking his prick... Janet only ever done this on sufferance, Sophie just once during the few times they had had the opportunity to make love, Charles saying, 'A man knows how it should feel. He knows what *he* wants... how could a woman do it as good as a man?'

Dennis aware that Charles was right.

About to release his sperm.

Needing to release his sperm.

Charles teasing.

Drawing back.

Till he begged...

Then, lying in the darkness. Down below, a succession of pizza delivery bikes arriving and departing, the riders revving their machines as they mounted the pavement... after a while, Charles saying, 'Now you.'

David saying, 'Do you have anything to drink in the flat?'

156

Charles saying, 'Sure, but it's on tap... it will need drawing.'
David not finding it funny.
Charles saying, 'We could butt-fuck?'
David saying, 'This was a mistake.'
Surprised by Charles's strength.
Charles saying, 'Bit late for second thoughts.'
David saying, *Jesus!*'

<h1 style="text-align:center">2</h1>

Eric Holtz, taken a long shower, used up every courtesy sachet in the bathroom, wearing a midnight-blue towelling dressing gown, watching early evening television, sipping absinthe, Czech import – 'Compliments of the house, Eric' – the bottle sent up by Harry, ran the Met Bar downstairs on the mezzanine floor of the hotel. Eric watching the woman on the television, talking down her Scottish accent. Holiday programme, Alaskan cruise liner, icebergs, killer whales, flight out to Fox Island, the woman saying, 'I feel so honoured... so lucky.' Eric agreeing, thinking, nice work if you can get it... Eric wondering how she would look without clothes, did she like to talk dirty, what was her expression when she fucked? Gritted teeth? Slack-mouthed? Eyes rolling back in her head? The emerald-green absinthe poured over brown sugar in a slotted spoon. Forget burning the sugar, setting alight the liquor in the glass... why burn off good alcohol? *La Fée Verte*, meeting point between madness, degeneracy and artistic genius, thujone competing with alcohol for hallucinogenic control of the neural synapsis...

Eric raising his glass.

Saying, '*Proust*, Harry.'

On the screen, now, a late middle-aged couple, out of place – should have been in Eastbourne – renting a villa in Mustique, saying how awfully nice the locals were... the cleaner, the gardener, the valet, the cook – all black and smiling. An English solicitor saying, 'Of course, at three thousand, five hundred pounds a week it's not *that* expensive if all the house-guests are contributing. Coming here as we have, just two couples, the children and a nanny, it does work out rather more.'

Then: 'Still, if one wants the best... one must be prepared to pay for it.'

Eric thinking, Fucking English.

Will they ever change?

Taking more absinthe.

His fourth glass.

Waiting for the woman...

No... not, the woman.

Not wishing to destroy the fantasy... the absinthe, the anticipation of the girl, mercifully, would clear his head of the fiasco with the refugees that he had got himself involved in, the deal coming apart at the seams. Romanians, Albanians, you name it, running around all over Kent, robbing, thieving, begging. His contact in Prague – midget, crazy bastard, Eric christened him Screw-Loose Lautrec – wanting to know what was going on. Eric quoting his favourite Englishman, Michael Caine, saying, 'Everybody got to be someplace.' Screw-Loose saying, 'Eric, we are dealing with the Russians, here, you perhaps do not understand that this is serious.' Eric thinking, The Russians? Guarantees? What fucking planet did they think they were on, coming over here playing hard-ball? Eric vowing that, from this moment on, he would stick to what he knew... art work, collectables, gentlemen doing business together in a civilised fashion... cosy world where two Constables could go missing from the V&A, sixteenth century Dutch paintings and a fifteenth century Italian master lost or stolen from Courtaulds, months before anybody realised what was going on...

Knock at the door.

The girl.

Picturing the last girl the agency sent... plump, grey school uniform with a short pleated skirt, stockings with ladders – lovely touch, the laddered stockings – eye liner and lipstick smudged, 36c bra, navy-blue bloomers...

Chubby.

Grubby.

Fingers...

Opening the door.

Surprised to see the two men back-lit by the wall-mounted light on the opposite wall... the first man stepping forward, taking hold of Eric, pulling his dressing gown down over his shoulders, trapping his arms, pushing Eric backwards into the room... The woman, clean-cut and peachy, back on the television, rounding off this week's programme, next week Simon Calder would be reporting from Agrigento in Sicily, Juliet Morris would be in New Orleans... Eric wondering if Miss Peachy had ever heard of the New Orleans 'Anything Goes' festival, gays from all over the United States descending on the city, parading around with their dongs hanging out, wanking off competitions on the old colonial wrought-iron balconies of Bourbon Street, crowds in the street below cheering... side-bets on which wanker would shoot his wad first. The second man stepping forward, plunging a knife into Eric's abdomen, just above the crutch, grasping the hilt in both hands, heaving upwards. Eric falling to his knees, intestines spilling onto the carpet.

Thinking, America...

Only, in America.

Schoolgirl standing in the door.

Screaming.

Could see up the schoolgirl's skirt.

Lace garter.

Thinking... guts for garters.

Shock closing down his life-support systems.

One by one...

Killing him with kindness.

3

Winston aware, now, that he was no longer bald, wide tread of dark hair – no sign of grey – traversing his skull from front to back, long enough now to tease upright with Brylcreem.

The Mohawkan...

Ate Mohicans for breakfast.

Wondering how soon before he could tie some braids, thread some ribbons and rings... whether face-paint would look good.

Falcon's feathers, what he needed. Where would you get falcon's feathers?

Going through the *Tai Chi* moves, watching himself in the triptych wall-mounted mirror, the two wings of the mirror angled to catch different perspectives. Winston showered and naked, enjoying the ripple of the tattoos, the bald eagle, the mountains, the flames, as he orchestrated the flow of energy, shifting from pose to pose, the musculature of his body the notes of a musical instrument, Winston a virtuoso musician, watching engorged arteries break surface, fan out across the surface of his body like tributaries across an alluvial flood plain…

The phone ringing.

Ignore it!

Concentration – the unqualified commitment and dedication to a single moment – broken… crossing to the bureau, lifting the receiver, Aurelie saying, 'You bastard!'

Winston saying, 'I warned you once.'

Then, knowing she hadn't: 'You found out.'

'Found out? Found out what?'

Thrown…

Now thinking, Another woman?

Worse…

What *could* be worse?

AIDS?

Preparing for a hammer blow that could change her life, bring definition to the abstract notion of her own future death. Winston smiling. Totally surprising her with the direction from which the hammer blow came. Teasing the moment before saying, 'That I'm your bastard brother.'

Aurelie hearing.

But *not* hearing.

Saying, 'What?!'

Winston saying, 'The brother your mother has been trying to locate all these years?'

Aurelie saying, 'You're a sick bastard.'

Then, 'You *are* joking?'

Then, 'Oh, my God.'

160

Winston saying, 'He won't help you.'

'Say it isn't true.'

'You've been fucking your big brother, Sis.'

'Oh, Christ!'

Then: 'Did you know... when we were doing it?'

'You think I'm a pervert?'

Still in view of the mirror, assuming a stance, one leg bent beneath him, the other fully stretched, buttocks grazing the floor, phone cradled to his ear, catching a three-quarter profile on the Mohawkan – *Oh, yes!* – saying to Aurelie, 'Why do you think I stopped coming round?'

Aurelie saying, 'Are you going to tell my mother?'

'Our mother?'

Again... 'Oh, Christ!'

'I was going to ask you the same thing.'

'It would break her heart.'

Then: 'She would blame herself.'

'It's tough all round.'

'Winston—'

'I'm hearing you.'

Winston knowing what Aurelie was thinking... that it was only words. How could only words make such a difference, hurt that much? Remembering his tenth birthday, Frank and Penny, The Scalextric Racing Car Set, Frank saying, 'We decided we would tell you on your tenth birthday.' Winston, early on, knowing how much only words could hurt.

Aurelie surprising him now, saying, 'Your rings and things.'

Winston saying, 'Aurelie, don't even think about it.'

Aurelie saying, 'What difference would it make, now?'

'I don't believe I'm hearing this.'

'I'm going to miss you.'

'Way it goes, Sis.'

Winston breaking the connection.

Closing in on the wall mirror... stalking his own image. Like a panther. Feeling too good to concentrate. Unable to empty his mind. Thinking about the dog called Caliban, the brittle *snap* as its neck broke, Eric Holtz and the fear in his eyes, the hotel security guard going down, Sophie – *his mother* – bringing herself off while Winston watched…

Cock hardening.

Deciding, yes…

Chest piece.

Giant bug… straight out of *Starship Troopers*.

Martian landscape.

Dry.

Arid.

Maybe a trooper in the bug's mandibles?

Legs gone.

Bleeding.

The phone ringing, again.

Winston, lifting the receiver, saying, 'What now, Aurelie?'

4

Yvonne, started the afternoon wearing a Reebok cross-back bra top and panelled shorts in matching burgundy wine, the matching bra and panties now mixed up somewhere in the sheets at the foot of the bed. Yvonne saying, 'When they're still alive – even when you're all grown up – you don't realise how important it is for you to impress them… make them proud of you.'

Then: 'It's a subliminal thing.'

Talking about the coach crash.

Jerez de la Frontera.

Spain.

Nineteen months… now.

Robert saying, 'But you weren't "all grown up".'

'Eighteen?'

Then: 'When I got the news there was this weird sense of relief. As if I was off the hook… freedom. Next minute, I was staring over the edge.'

'What edge?'

'The big abyss… next in line.'

Robert saying, again, 'Eighteen?'

'Age isn't how long you've had, it's how long you have left… my parents were in their late-thirties when they died.'

162

'Is that why you do what you do?'

'Do *what* do I do?'

'Table dance.'

'Table *side* dance.'

'All right.'

'There is a difference.'

The one time Yvonne had taken a lap dancing gig – what the fuck, it couldn't be *that* bad – converted pub in Banham Street, Hammersmith, NEON NIGHTS, used to be called the Bricklayers' Arms, pool table, old geezers playing dominoes... drunken woman, size of a beluga whale, screaming, 'Get your syphilitic arse off my husband!'

No, thank you.

Robert saying, 'Would you be doing it... they were still alive?'

'I got nobody left to impress.'

'How about me?'

'It might come as a surprise, Robert... not all table side dancers are orphans.'

Digging out the Reebok bra and panties from the bottom of the bed, saying, 'Sixty notes... six dances.'

Robert saying, 'We going to be staying in bed *all* the time?'

Yvonne saying, 'You have a better idea?'

5

That afternoon with Sophie, The Doves, Fuller's pub along the river at Hammersmith, in all the tourist guide books, Sophie a gin and tonic, Winston orange juice, saying to the barman, 'This fresh? I don't drink reconstituted.' The bar staff clearing up after the lunchtime trade, Winston and Sophie both eating Ploughman's Salad – Stilton cheese – from the all-day buffet in the back bar... too cold to sit outside by the river.

Sophie saying, 'This is nice.'

Winston saying, 'You say so.'

Then: 'Another G&T?'

Sophie saying, 'One is more than enough.'

Eight days, now, since she had touched anything...

Temazepam.

163

Valium.

Librium.

Couldn't believe how good she was feeling... Sophie dressed up for the occasion – first time out in public with Winston – wearing a raspberry bubble jacket over a ribbed polo-neck, grey drawstring woollen skirt... Winston – concession to Sophie – not wearing the motorcycle security chain round his neck, wondering if Sophie ever intended to tell him what Aurelie had told him over the telephone this morning...

About David.

Aurelie saying: 'As her son,' – not, her lover – 'I thought you had a right to know.'

Later, walking back along the Mall, Sophie shopping in Chiswick High Road, greengrocer stall outside Marks & Spencer, Sophie paying for an aubergine, the stall-holder saying, 'All right for batteries, are you, love?' Winston saying, further down the road, 'You have to put up with that?' Sophie saying, 'I love being out with you... places I can't touch you the way I want to touch you.'

Then: 'Do people always look at you like this? The double-take? Not catching your eye... like they were afraid?'

Winston saying, 'They know what's good for them.'

'You're a big kid.'

Winston thinking, *Your* big kid.

'You going to mother me?'

Wondering about David.

What he was going to do to him... and why.

Because Sophie was his mother?

Lover?

Both?

Saying, 'Nothing wrong with respect.'

'It's not respect... it's fear.'

'Same difference.'

'You think so?'

Winston saying, 'Sophie' – talking about the tattoo – 'On my back-piece it says, FUCK WITH ME!'

Sophie saying, taking Winston's arm, 'Don't I just.'

... sudden image of Jim.

164

Jim saying, 'There's one in every band. Fucks anything that moves.'

Then: 'I was never that one, Sophie.'

Questions she wanted to ask Winston.

Couldn't.

Saying, now, 'I have a secret.'

Busker, on the pavement outside Woolworths, playing one note on a penny whistle, could still recognise 'Jingle Bells' from the timing. Sophie giving him 20p. Winston saying, 'Fucker ought to learn to play that.' Then, 'I've got a secret, too.'

Sophie saying, 'You won't like my secret.'

Winston saying, 'You're not going to like my secret, either.'

Picturing how it would be – cat bringing in the mouse? – when he told Sophie... after the event, said, 'David... I did him.'

Matter of fact.

Sophie saying, 'What do you mean, "Did him"?'

Winston saying, 'Aurelie told me.'

Sophie saying, 'Told you *what*?'

Winston imagining the whole scenario...

His secret still intact.

Sophie saying, now, 'Can we get a cab?'

'Home?'

'Your place... right now.'

Winston saying, 'No can do.'

'You're teasing?'

'Something on.'

'Something on?'

Winston saying, 'Sophie, I'm not in the habit of repeating myself.'

6

Anyone who was anybody at Club 67, apart from Dennis The Diceman, knew all about Boxey Carter's practical joke – twenty-five years, now – every once in a blue moon Boxey slipping an extra key, Chubb, Yale, Mul-T-Lock, whatever, onto Dennis's key-ring... Dennis, so many keys in the first place, lock-up garages all over west London – what would you expect – never noticed when a new key was added to the ring. Boxey estimated, at the last count, Dennis The Diceman was walking around with upward of thirty assorted keys…

Fuck all use to Dennis.

Weighing down the pocket of his trenchcoat.

Dennis, now, saying – why everybody was thinking about the key-ring… Boxey's practical joke – 'Fulham… right. Rented it in the '60s for six bob a week. Bought it leasehold for three hundred and fifty, mid-'70s. Sold it last week… how much?'

Beryl saying, 'Retirement fund looking healthy?'

'Hazard a guess.'

Bobby-Boy, the only one not listening.

Out of it, already.

Charlie saying, 'Why don't I run you home?'

Bobby-Boy saying, 'Why don't you fuck off.'

Beryl saying, 'Yellow card!'

Boxey saying, 'Make it a red… put the miserable fucker out of his misery.'

Dennis The Diceman saying, 'Sixteen thousand, five hundred pounds…'

Lock-up garage.

Off Munster Road.

Dennis, raising his glass, saying, 'Here's to CPZ.'

Controlled Parking Zones.

Charlie, raising his own glass, saying, 'The telephone only rings once… right, Dennis?'

'Something like that, Charlie.'

Then: 'Should have seen this prat… comes in with, "Fifteen will have to be my final offer." I'm saying, "Final offer? You already made your final offer… I'm just here for the paperwork." Meanwhile, he's saying to the missus – could have given *her* one, no uncertain terms – "How many *leaves*, Nancy…? You didn't forget the rocket?"

'Talking about a salad, for fuck's sake.

'"Expecting company?" I say.

'The prat says, "I was merely seeking to establish a platform for negotiation."

166

'His wife saying, "I have this white truffle oil, Cuneo, I found it in Sainsbury's… you think I should use that?"'

'I'm saying, "If you've lost interest?"'

'He's saying, "Look… let's talk."'

'Then: "The Beaune-Gréves, it is breathing, darling?"'

'I say: "Very nice, too… I like a nice Burgundy." '

Then: 'What a cunt!'

Beryl saying, 'Yellow card!'

Dennis saying, 'Sonja!'

Charlie saying, 'I could never bring myself to say that word.'

Boxey saying, 'What word?'

'C-U-N-T'

'Cunt?'

'Boxey!'

'You spell it out?'

Then: 'C-U-N-T?'

'Wrong with that?'

Charlie, thinking about it, then saying, 'How would *you* spell C-U-N-T?'

Beryl saying, 'Profound.'

Boxey saying, 'Would I take it, Dennis, that this is the first step in a downsizing exercise—'

'In the modern vernacular.'

'… towards early retirement?'

Dennis saying, 'Hands off cocks… on socks!'

'More like the other way round, Dennis.'

Noticing Bobby-Boy had disappeared.

Boxey saying, 'What happened to Bobby-Boy?'

Dennis saying, 'Has to be in a bad way…'

Beryl saying, 'That hand looked nasty.'

'Not a dicky-bird about the four and a half I owe him.'

Then: 'How did he do it anyway?'

Charlie, surprising himself, saying, 'You're asking the wrong person, Dennis.'

Boxey saying, 'Get him.'

Dennis saying, 'All of a sudden.'

167

Winston, calling her at home, getting her out of bed, telling Sophie how he found David Cornish, put him in the Accident & Emergency ward, Charing Cross Hospital, severe concussion, broken jaw, double compound fracture of his right arm below the elbow, various minor contusions and bleeding...

Started at the junction with Turnham Green Terrace – no particular reason, had to start somewhere – heading west along the High Street, calling in at each pub, standing not too close, but with a clear view of the bar area, calling the pub number on his mobile... hearing the phone ringing behind the bar, watching the bar staff ignore the call, hoping it would go away, talking to customers, serving drinks, sharing a joke, finally, one of them pulling a face, picking up.

Saying, 'George the Fourth.'

'Windmill.'

'All Bar One.'

Winston saying, 'Could you put out a call for a David Cornish?'

The barman saying, 'We don't accept private calls on this line. There's a public phone in the bar takes incoming calls.'

Winston saying, 'It's his son... motorcycle accident.'

The barman saying, 'Oh, I'm sorry... just a minute.'

Winston watching as the barman placed the receiver on the counter-top, turned to the pub, shouted, 'David Cornish! Is there a David Cornish in tonight?'

Coming back, picking up the receiver, saying, 'Sorry, no luck. Have you tried—'

Winston, already out the door.

Moving on to the next pub.

At the Old Packhorse, corner of Acton Lane, leading up to Chiswick Park Station, the barman picking up, no objection to taking a private call, saying, 'Hold a moment.'

Calling out the name.

David Cornish.

A man in his early-fifties, thinning hair, check sports jacket, cavalry twill trousers, brown brogues – Winston thinking, *Him*?

For fuck's sake! – approaching the bar, his step too deliberate to be sober, taking the receiver, saying to the barman, 'Who is it?'

The barman saying, 'No idea.'

Winston saying, 'David Cornish?'

'That's right.'

'I have a message from Sophie.'

'From Sophie?'

'Can you meet her?'

'Meet her? Where?'

'You know the Crown... Chiswick High Road?'

'I know the Crown.'

Then: 'When?'

Winston saying, 'Now.'

'Now?'

'You have something better to do?'

'Sorry?'

'Is that a problem?'

'No... it's just—'

Winston breaking the connection.

Watching David Cornish hand back the receiver to the barman, saying, 'Thank you.' Going back to his table, standing to finish his pint... walking past Winston, pushing open the door, Winston following him out onto the pavement, saying, 'Excuse me.'

David turning round.

Not yet afraid.

Saying, 'Sorry?'

Confused.

Trying to place the voice.

Why so familiar?

Winston saying, 'You have a light?'

David saying, 'No.'

Then: 'I don't smoke.'

Winston thinking, Why do they always have to tell you that? As if anyone *gave* a fuck.

Saying, 'I don't, either.'

David saying, 'If this is a pick-up, you've made a big mistake.'

169

Winston saying, 'Pick-up?'

Then: 'You think I'm a queer?'

…making it *that* easy.

David saying, 'The Gay Gordons… they call it the Happy Gordons now. Did you know that?'

Then: 'Rum old world.'

… Sophie, listening on the phone, saying, 'That easy?'

Winston saying, 'That easy.'

'You put him in hospital… broke his arm in *two* places?'

Winston saying, 'Snap!'

Then: 'Snap!'

8

Bobby-Boy and the girl shivering on the balcony, vicious draught coming down the hall from the open front door, wind trap between Charlie's block and Hammersmith Town Hall, coming straight in off the bend in the Thames, Bobby-Boy saying, 'Brandy schnapps. Office Christmas party… Rhoda doesn't normally drink.'

Charlie saying, 'Christmas?'

'Only three weeks away, Charlie.'

The girl saying, 'Rhonda… it's Rhonda, with the "n".'

'Sorry… Rhonda.'

Rhonda saying, 'You live here?'

'Don't be daft.'

'Is there a bathroom?'

Bobby-Boy saying, 'Charlie?'

Charlie saying, 'You know what time it is?'

Then: 'It's two o'clock in the morning, Bobby-Boy.'

'What are friends for?'

'You tell me.'

Charlie pointing to the door, right of the hall, saying to Rhonda, 'In there.'

Rhonda saying, 'You two just going to stand there listening?'

Then: 'Girl needs *some* privacy.'

Bobby-Boy saying, 'You going to invite us in, or what?'

Charlie standing aside to let them pass.

Then closing the front door.

Bobby-Boy saying, 'Fuck, it's cold in here.'

'Wasn't a minute ago.'

In the living room, Charlie saying, 'Why are you doing this?'

Bobby-Boy thinking, She was there, Charlie.

She was just *there*.

Saying: 'Fuck knows… I don't even fancy it.'

Sound of the toilet chain pulling.

Cistern flushing.

Charlie thinking, That will please the neighbours, this time of night, old bag downstairs always going on…

Not one thing.

It was another.

Rhonda coming into the front room, taken off her hooded top, adjusting her knickers beneath the slacks, slim-fit blue with white piping, matching blue navel stud showing between the trouser waist and a red fatigue top. Charlie wondering why all women nowadays dressed like they were just back from some track event at White City Stadium… no idea what was meant to look good on a woman…

Thinking, What's new?

Rhonda saying, 'This is where you are.'

Bobby-Boy saying, 'We needed a bed… I thought, My mate, Charlie, has a spare room.'

'It's not a spare room. It's my mother's bedroom.'

Rhonda saying, 'Do I get to meet your mother?'

Bobby-Boy saying, 'She's been dead ten years.'

Rhonda saying, 'Weird.'

Bobby-Boy saying, 'Well?'

Charlie saying, 'You can't use my mother's bedroom.'

Then: 'Have my room… I'll get my head down on the settee.'

Bobby-Boy saying, 'Your room? You must be joking? When was the last time you changed the sheets in there?'

Rhonda saying, 'Boys! Boys!'

Then: 'Anything to drink?'

Charlie saying, 'Sorry.'

Had enough.

Not even going to suggest a cup of tea.

Coffee…

Rhonda, looking at Bobby-Boy – as if she was seeing him for the first time – saying, 'You know, there's some people… you can't imagine what they would look like in the daylight. You're one of them.'

'How am I supposed to take that?'

'Take it how you like.'

Then: 'I'm going to be sick.'

Charlie saying, 'Jes-us!'

Bobby-Boy saying, 'You know where it is.'

Then: 'Don't miss the bowl.'

Bobby-Boy and Charlie, standing in Charlie's living room, listening to Rhonda throwing up in the toilet, didn't have time to close the living room or toilet door. Bobby-Boy saying, 'Mongolian… as much as you can eat for a tenner. Never a good idea on top of booze.'

Charlie saying, again, 'Why are you doing this, Bobby-Boy?'

'Well, Rhonda's got a husband and I've got a wife.'

'I didn't mean that.'

'Don't start giving me all that shit about Toyah being such a wonderful woman, and how she doesn't deserve this.'

Then: 'Who was she fucking, Charlie?'

Charlie saying, 'I don't know.'

'So, she *was* fucking somebody?'

'I didn't say that.'

'You didn't have to.'

Could hear Rhonda splashing water on her face.

Cleaning her teeth.

Charlie thinking, Not my fucking toothbrush!

Bobby-Boy saying to Rhonda, when she came back in, 'I'm putting you in a cab… where shall I say?'

Rhonda saying, 'That might not be such a bad idea.'

'Well?'

'Pinner.'

'Pinner? Where the fuck is Pinner?'

Charlie saying, 'Off the edge of the known universe, Bobby-Boy.'

Bobby-Boy saying to Charlie, 'How are you for cash?'
Then: 'You going to tell me, or what?'
Charlie saying, 'Life's too short, Bobby-Boy.'
Bobby-Boy saying…
Straight away.
'Fuck me.'
Then: 'Winston.'

chapter eleven

'Go long! Go long!'

1

Club 67.

Everybody talking about Dennis The Diceman.

His sudden demise…

Third whisky and water of the afternoon, Dennis, usual stool at the bar, saying – to anyone could be bothered listening – 'Says here,' reading from the paper, *'The working class is reviled for its incurable racism, but no other social group has dealt with genuine racial integration.'*

Charlie Paul saying, 'Over my head, Dennis.'

Dennis saying, 'What it means, Charlie, it means the working class is where it always has been and where it always will be… on the front line.'

Beryl saying, 'Don't get your testosterones all in a twist.'

Boxey saying, 'Chance would be a fine thing.'

Charlie saying, 'What about the middle classes?'

Dennis saying, 'What *about* the middle classes?'

Saying: 'The middle classes never had a problem with integration … and I'll tell you for why… Because there is nothing more middle class than a middle class Black.'

Standing up.

Clutching his right arm.

Saying, 'Fuck me… lights out!'

Crashing to the floor.

As Beryl put it, later... stone cold dead.

Charlie saying, 'It takes a while for a body to grow cold, Beryl.'

Beryl saying, 'Figure of speech, Charlie.'

Then: 'Weird, right? It was Boxey just underwent the multiple bypass operation, yet it's Dennis who dies of a heart attack.'

Charlie saying, 'Not so weird if you think about it.'

Beryl saying, 'Bobby-Boy know?'

Charlie nodding, not wishing to recount the conversation...

Bobby-Boy saying, 'Fucking tragedy.'

Then: 'Four and a half big ones out the window.'

The Clarice Cliff money.

'Less forty.'

'Less forty?'

'Dennis advanced you for the clamp, or did you forget?'

Bobby-Boy saying, 'Oh, fuck off, Charlie.'

Charlie saying, to Beryl, 'It hasn't been Bobby-Boy's week.'

Beryl saying, 'It hasn't been Dennis's week, either.'

Carrying on with the story.

Just Charlie at the bar... '60s DJ, in early, setting up the sound system for the evening, 10cc, 'I'm Not In Love,' the vocalist repeating over and over: *Big boys don't cry, Big boys don't cry.* Charlie remembering Bobby-Boy saying he liked 10cc for their lyrics...

Big boys don't cry?

Oh, do fuck off.

Were they taking the piss, or what?

Beryl saying, 'There was Boxey, down on his knees next to Dennis, Dennis making strange noises in his throat, Boxey saying, "Stand by your beds, right, Dennis?"'

Bursting into tears.

Beryl saying, 'No *ordinary* tears.'

Then: 'Not mate's tears.'

'How do you mean?'

'*Lover's* tears.'

Charlie saying, 'Lover's tears?'

175

Then: 'The Diceman and Boxey?'

'Makes sense, you think about it.'

Charlie still vacant.

Beryl saying, 'They were a *couple*, Charlie.'

Charlie saying, 'Course they were a couple… like that, Dennis and Boxey.'

'No, Charlie… a couple couple.'

Charlie falling in.

Saying: 'Dennis and Boxey? Turd burglars?'

Beryl saying, 'You always did have a way with words, Charlie.'

10cc still on the sound system.

'I'm Not In Love.'

Big boys don't cry.

Charlie going over to the DJ, waiting till he removed his headphones, saying, 'What do they call you, kid?'

The DJ saying, 'Pete.'

Charlie saying, 'Give me the record, Pete.'

Pete saying, 'How come?'

Charlie saying, 'Nobody wants to hear it.'

Then: 'You have a problem with that?'

2

Bobby-Boy coming awake, Toyah beside him in the bed, perched on one elbow, saying, 'That hurt?'

Bobby-Boy saying, 'Fuck do you care?'

Holding up the bandaged hand.

Taking a while to remember why it *was* bandaged.

Saying: 'This is your doing.'

Toyah saying, 'You *really* thought I was fucking Charlie Paul?'

Then: 'You're drinking too much, you know that, don't you, Bobby-Boy?'

'Tell me about it.'

Toyah saying, 'That trip to Guernsey… you still up for it?'

'Fuck you talking about?'

'I got the money, Bobby-Boy.'

'I'm not with you?'

'The eighteen thousand, three hundred pounds?'

'You took the eighteen thousand, three hundred pounds?'

'Is there any other money?'

'Fucking bitch!'

'Lying there, boot wide open, somebody had to take it. I figured it might as well be me.'

'I don't believe this.'

Then: 'Eighteen thousand, *three* hundred? You're light. What happened to the other four hundred?'

'Girl needs to look presentable, she's going on a trip.'

Bobby-Boy sitting up, pushing back the duvet, swinging his legs off the bed. Feeling like shit. Vowing he would never touch another drop, thinking, Fuck do you think you're kidding, saying, 'Charlie, was he in on this?'

Toyah, not moving, letting Bobby-Boy see just how good she still looked, running one foot against the calf of her other leg in case Bobby-Boy missed the point, saying, feeling guilty as she said it, 'Is Charlie in on anything?'

Bobby-Boy saying, 'He knew about you and Winston.'

Toyah saying, 'Me and Winston?'

Then: 'Charlie tell you that?'

'Not in so many words.'

Toyah sitting up in the bed.

Saying; 'Let's clear the air here, Bobby-Boy. Is there anybody out there you *don't* think I've been fucking?'

Bobby-Boy's eyes on Toyah's boobs. Toyah remembering him saying, 'How come you're in your mid-thirties, can still pass the pencil test?' Toyah saying, 'You're a crude fucking bastard.' Bobby-Boy saying, now, 'The tattoo.'

'The tattoo?'

'The budgie.'

'The kakapo.'

Then; 'That's it? You think I've been fucking Winston Capaldi because I've had a kakapo tattooed on my butt?'

Then: 'You are one sad fucker, Bobby-Boy.'

Then: 'I blame the upbringing.'

Bobby-Boy saying, 'I'm having trouble with this, Toyah. First

177

you're leaving, then you're stealing my money... then you're giving it back. The fuck is going on?'

Toyah, standing now, saying, 'I never wanted to end up like this.'

Bobby-Boy saying, 'Like what?'

Toyah saying, 'Just somebody's wife.'

Bobby-Boy saying, 'You're fucking crazy, you know that?'

Then, 'I ought to smack you one, what you've put me through.'

Toyah saying, 'Hey! Could this be a breakthrough in our relationship?'

3

Yvonne telling Robert, 'As part of the training you lay there for four hours, six hen's eggs various places on your body, the instructor dropping ice cubes on you... you move once, one of those eggs falls off, the instructor resets the timer, you start all over again.'

Talking about *Nyotamori*.

Literally, the adorned body of a woman.

Yvonne read in a magazine, Japanese business executives willing to pay 150,000 yen – seven hundred pounds – to eat their sushi off the naked body of a Nyotamori geisha... blue marlin, squid, tuna, scallops, sea urchin prepared with raw egg, all on beds of vinegar-soaked rice, vine leaves and flower decoration covering the geisha's genitals.

Yvonne saying, 'You have to shave all your body hair, armpits waxed, wash with unscented soap, then a very hot douche and an ice cold shower so you don't sweat... four hours, all that takes. Every time.'

Then: 'You imagine... having to lie there, motionless, while some geriatric old pervert is poking around where he shouldn't with a pair of chopsticks.'

Then: 'And you can't move... no matter what happens... even if they throw up over you.'

Robert saying, 'So you're thinking of a job change?'

'You have to be a virgin.'

Then: 'Besides, I think I'll stick with table side dancing.'

178

Robert saying, 'Seven hundred pounds is a lot of money.'

Yvonne saying, 'You don't think the geishas get that, do you?'

'You could start your own business... all the go now, sushi.'

Yvonne saying, 'Want to practice?'

'How do you mean?'

'Me with a Big Mac on each titty... pizza wedge on my fanny?'

Robert saying, 'What kind of pizza?'

4

Aurelie screaming at Sophie.

Sophie saying, 'I can understand you being upset.'

Then: 'Your ex and everything.'

Couldn't help herself...

Feeling smug.

Aurelie saying, 'No! You *don't* understand. You don't understand *anything*!'

Aurelie and Sophie standing either side of the kitchen table, Sophie in her kimono dressing gown, Aurelie wearing a pale blue flannel dress, mohair knitted trim – wonders would never cease – going for a job interview, Cussons and Knight, Estate Agent on the Chiswick High Road, needed an administrative coordinator, smartly presented, willing to work flexible hours. Aurelie finding the ad under situations vacant in the *Brentford & Chiswick*.

Sophie saying, 'Eat your breakfast.'

Then: 'You're going to be late.'

Two bowls of cornflakes, Sainsbury's own brand, on the table, Sophie's with a sliced banana – part of her 'high fibre diet' – Aurelie saying, 'Eat my breakfast?'

Sophie saying, 'It's not as if you two were still an item.'

Thinking about David...

What Winston had done to him.

Charing Cross Hospital... concussion, broken jaw, fractured right arm below the elbow, the doctors still not sure how much mobility David would have in the arm once the plaster came off.

Winston expecting Sophie to be grateful.

Like a big child.

179

Aurelie saying, 'And would it interest you to know just *why* we're not still an item?'

Sophie saying, 'I'm not sure if Winston and I are an item, either... not after David.'

Aurelie, sitting down at the table, saying, 'I couldn't tell you... I really couldn't tell you.'

Lighting a cigarette.

Blowing smoke towards the chrome light fitting above the table.

Sophie saying, 'You know I hate you doing that.'

Aurelie not able to resist. Looking up at her mother, still standing, saying, 'You're fucking your own son... and you come down on me for *smoking?*'

5

Green Carnation, Richmond.

Bobby-Boy getting them in – what's new? – OJ, no ice, for Winston, half of lager on tap him and Charlie Paul, too early for any serious drinking, Patrick just opened the doors. Bobby-Boy intrigued by what Winston would have to say for himself... he wanted to clear the air, that was fine by Bobby-Boy. Charlie Paul, his fat arse perched on a bar stool, lifting one cheek, farting, saying, 'Tails!' Surprised nobody found it amusing. Bobby-Boy saying, 'Charlie, you truly are a disgusting specimen of humanity.' Patrick, behind the bar, serving the drinks, taking Bobby-Boy's money, bloke along the bar – only other customer – rattling his small change, Patrick saying, 'With you one second, Frank,' nodding towards the guitar case at Winston's feet, saying, 'Going to give us a tune then, Winston?'

Frank, early fifties, long ginger hair, thin on top, Zapata moustache, faded jeans and cowboy boots, still rattling his small change, moving closer, saying – to Winston's back – 'Don't mind me asking... what kind of guitar you got in there?'

Then: 'Reason I ask... used to play a bit, myself.'

Bobby-Boy saying, 'Didn't we all.'

Winston, turning towards Frank, saying, 'Fender Telecaster, natural wood finish, circa 1972.'

Frank, saying to Patrick, 'Pint of Strongbow, if you would.'

Then, to Winston, 'Worth a bit, that, you know.'

Winston saying, 'Fiver.'

'Fiver?'

'Yours for a fiver.'

Smiling at Bobby-Boy.

Frank saying, 'You know what you're doing?'

Bobby-Boy saying, 'Fucked if I do.'

Winston saying, 'I know what I'm doing.'

Patrick passing Frank his pint of cider.

Frank saying, 'Mind if I take a look?'

Winston saying, 'Help yourself.'

Frank opening the guitar case across two bar stools, taking out the Telecaster, running one finger across the open strings, saying, 'Recognise that? Opening chord of "A Hard Day's Night". All the music critics wanking on about pentatonic clusters... all Lennon did was strum the open chord... pure genius.'

Winston saying, 'You want the guitar or not?'

Frank, closing the case, taking out a five pound note, saying, 'I'm not going to ask where this came from.'

Winston saying, 'Smart boy.'

Taking the fiver.

Bobby-Boy taking the fiver from Winston's hand.

Saying: 'Mine, I believe.'

Charlie Paul saying, 'I don't get any of this.'

Bobby-Boy saying, 'Do you ever?'

Winston saying, to Frank, 'You still here, Frank?'

6

Sophie, once more, stuck in front of the yoghurt shelves, Sainsbury's, Chiswick Branch, knowing now that there would be no Jim to come along and rescue her, appear at the end of the shopping aisle, throw a four-pack of Danone Chocolate Mousse – whatever – into her trolley, say, 'These will do for a change.' Sophie thinking, If I had a pet – a cat, or a dog – would I suffer from pet food catatonia too?

Thinking... that last record company launch that Jim went to–

was invited to – after the record company had ditched him, the A&R man saying, '*Afterthought*? Great name for a last album, Jim.' What a joker *he* was… the reception held at the Pump House, converted Victorian water-works building off the Fulham Palace Road, near the river. Jim pissed on Jack Daniel's, describing the party as, 'All dry ice, disco, and tarts with their tits hanging out.'

Saying: 'You spend your life going, "I'll show 'em… I'll give the fuckers what for." Then you think, Show 'em? Show who? Show them what? Why am I busting my balls off like this… all for nothing?'

Sophie coming down from the bedroom – she had been reading, not asleep, *The Unbearable Lightness of Being*, Milan Kundera – making them both a cup of tea, saying to Jim, 'You want some toast… biscuits?' Then saying, 'But it's what you do. It's what you enjoy doing.'

'Not any more.'

'Then do something else.'

'Like what?'

Then: 'I can't hack it with this new breed of rock journo. Think they're so fucking cool just because they've heard of Marmalade.'

Then: 'This rock chick tonight… asks me if I know Steve Marriott, and, "How's he doing?" This is the same bitch who wrote a feature in *London Live* about the late, great Captain Beefheart. Beefheart rings her up at the magazine, all the way from California, says, "Hey, I'm Captain Beefheart. I'm here to tell you that I'm very much alive." She says, "You can't be Captain Beefheart. Captain Beefheart is dead." The ultimate fascism, right? I think, therefore it is so.'

'Religion has been getting away with that for centuries.'

'Don't go intellectual on me, Sophie.'

Sophie saying, 'Drink your tea, Jim.'

Jim saying, 'And then this other dipshit chimes in… says, "So how come you never made it big… I mean, really big?"'

'I say, "Because I was too arrogant. Thought I was too good to have to play the game. Later, I realised… Sinatra, The Beatles, Bob Dylan, even they weren't *that* good."'

Then: 'That's when you *know* you're losing it… when you try to hold a serious conversation with a rock journalist.

'The dipshit says, "What about Presley?"

'I say, "Where would Presley be today if he hadn't made Blue Hawaii?"

'Smart-arse says, "Alive?"

'I say, "Fuck difference would that make to you?"

'Right over their heads, that one went.'

Then, Jim saying, ' "Jim Grace? The Crunch? Should I have heard of you?" The new credo… I have not heard of you, ergo, you do not exist.'

Pride.

Taking a terrible beating…

At the hands of children.

Sophie saying, 'You're very drunk, Jim.'

Jim saying, about Steve Marriott, 'Fucking bitch probably missed the news while her mother was changing titty.'

Jim saying, when the illness came, when the multiple sclerosis was diagnosed, 'In a way it's a relief.'

'I'm not with you?'

'An excuse.'

Then: 'The heat's on, but the pressure's off.'

This, before either Sophie or Jim had any comprehension of what lay ahead…

Jim at the kitchen table.

After the record company launch.

Saying, 'Could have been worse.'

Then: 'Imagine… having an ice cream named after you.'

Cherry Garcia…

Sainsbury's.

Chiswick Branch.

Sophie selecting a four-pack of Bio yoghurt. Black cherry, strawberry, rhubarb and vanilla.

Thinking: How else would they sell vanilla?

Except in a mixed four-pack.

Always the one left in the fridge.

Past its sell-by date.

Looking towards the end of the aisle…

No Jim.

Not even a ghost.

Charlie Paul coming up the alley, bag of chips from Costa's, salt, plenty of malt vinegar, hands warming on the chip bag, seeing Winston standing outside Club 67… waiting. Not for Beryl to check him out on the newly installed CCTV, press the door release, let him into the club…

Winston, not even rang the bell.

Spoken on the intercom.

Just waiting.

For Charlie.

Winston saying, 'I've a bone to pick.'

Charlie saying, 'Chip?'

Holding out the bag.

Then: 'What's that on your face?'

'War paint.'

Charlie saying, 'Oh, fuck!'

Couldn't help himself.

Dropping the chips, turning, running back down the alley towards the shop lights of Turnham Green Terrace, everything open late in the run up to Christmas. Charlie going right, towards Turnham Green Station, colliding with a stack of Christmas trees, the galvanised iron funnel they used to wrap the trees, flower stall under the railway bridge. Charlie walking fast now – not running – not daring to look back, knowing if he saw Winston behind him, caught his eye…

He would stop.

Roll over…

And die.

In the station entrance, crowd of commuters coming down the stairs, west-bound District Line train already pulling out over the bridge, bottle-neck at the ticket booth, Charlie forcing his way through, ticket collector shouting after him… top of the stairs now, nobody on the platform, all on the west-bound train heading for Ealing… looking back. Winston coming up the stairs, all the time in the world, hands tight round either end of the motor-cycle security chain… still hung round his neck.

Piccadilly Line train, east-bound, heading into town, thundering through on the farthest of the two central tracks, then another Piccadilly train in the opposite direction, faces passing in a blur of light, Charlie feeling the drag of the slipstream pulling him towards the edge of the platform, thinking, Catch the fucker off balance…

One good shove.

Then thinking, Charlie, Charlie!

In your dreams.

Saying, 'Winston.'

Then: 'Why?'

Winston saying, 'Because you ran.'

'Bastard, right?'

Winston coming up the last step.

Saying, 'Don't make it any harder.'

Charlie saying, 'Life… it's a bastard.'

Winston laughing.

'Lot of bottle, Charlie.

'I'll give you that.'

8

Dennis's wake.

Four bedroom semi-detached mock-Tudor in West Ealing, Dennis had shared the house with Boxey – white shag carpet, chintzy wallpaper, gold and brass fittings, tassels hanging from everything except the Steinway. Bobby-Boy at the French windows looking out over the expanse of crazy-paved patio, well tended lawn and borders, garden shed at the far end, almost hidden by a weeping willow… Detective Chief Inspector Alec Diaper telling Bobby-Boy, 'This is social… not business.' Schooner of medium dry amontillado sherry in one hand, slice of Marks & Spencer lemon drizzle cake on a patterned tea plate in the other. Saying to Bobby-Boy, 'You'll excuse me if I don't offer to shake hands.'

Bobby-Boy with a large scotch and ice.

Cut glass tumbler.

Saying: 'Diaper? Is that for real?'

DCI Diaper saying, 'There are five of us in the local phone book.'

'All full of shit?'

'I was hoping we might avoid that kind of comment.'

'Like they say, hope springs eternal.'

DCI Diaper saying, 'There was a recent survey... it showed that children with names likely to cause them social embarrassment become above-average achievers.'

'So what went wrong?'

Then: 'I knew a girl called Placenta, once... hippy parents, child of the '60s. Two kids by the age of fifteen. Crank, crack, smack... you name it, she did it. Hopeless case from day one.'

'You know that song... "Boy Named Sue"?'

'Johnny Cash.'

'On the button. Father calls his son Sue. Figures it will toughen the boy up, all the stick he will have to put up with, going through life with a name like Sue.'

'I know the story.'

'Years later, catches up with his old man in a low-life bar, kicks all kinds of shit out of him, his old man telling him, "Son, no way could you have bested me, I hadn't called you Sue".'

Bobby-Boy saying, 'Great song.'

DCI Diaper saying, 'At school they used to call me Spot.'

Bobby-Boy saying, 'Why are we having this conversation?'

Seeing Beryl across the room, looking good in a black dress, scoop neck, string of pearls, engaged in conversation with a man, younger than Dennis, mid-fifties, something about the expression, could have been a brother... Bobby-Boy realising he knew nothing about Dennis, outside of small talk at the club, business they conducted.

Thinking, Too fucking late, now.

DCI Diaper saying, 'Came from "Nappy Rash".'

'What?'

'Spot.'

Bobby-Boy saying, 'Shouldn't there have been a rhyme in

186

there, somewhere? You know, like butcher's... as in, butcher's hook, look? Micky Most... toast?'

'You mean, rash... as in, rhymes with cash?'

Then: 'As in, Clarice Cliff cash?'

'And they say all coppers are thick.'

'As two planks... but, you're not one of them, are you, Bobby-Boy?'

'Know thine enemy.'

Bobby-Boy remembering his old man quoting Marlon, *Godfather I*, scene in the garden with Michael... Keep your friends close, but your enemies closer. Realising he was long overdue a visit to the nursing home – despite his old man could no longer tell him apart from the gardener, poor old sod – help him with his Christmas cards, writing and sending them off.

Saying...

Why should he feel proud?

'My old man taught me that.'

His old man... remembering how much he had loved him, idolised him, when he was a kid... the first crack, the first chink in the solid brick wall of that unconditional love... Bobby-Boy and his father standing on the platform at Stamford Brook station waiting for a District Line train, going to the museums, South Kensington – must have been a Sunday afternoon – Bobby-Boy's father holding Bobby-Boy's hand, telling him not to stand too near the edge, telling him that when lorries wanted to drive down the railway track, all the lorry driver had to do was take the rubber tyres off, run on the rims. For years after that, Bobby-Boy looking to see a lorry driving down the railway track... finally realising that his old man had lied to him.

Made a joke.

At Bobby-Boy's expense.

Now, it was, 'You should see my son, planted all those trees, he did.'

Alzheimer's.

Stage Four...

Saying to DCI Diaper, 'Do's like this, what can you say that hasn't already been said?'

'A million times.'

'Exactly. There are moments in life when everything comes out sounding like a platitude... funerals being a case in question.'

'At least he didn't suffer. Life goes on. Perhaps it's for the best?'

Bobby-Boy saying, 'He would have liked that.'

'There... that's another.'

'No... you bending my ear. Dennis's funeral. Warped sense of humour, our Dennis.'

Boxey circulating amongst the mourners, freshening drinks, wearing an expensive charcoal-grey double-breasted suit, high shine on his shoes, Bobby-Boy willing to bet he had polished the soles especially for the occasion – last of a breed – DCI Diaper saying to Bobby-Boy, 'We're going to miss Dennis.'

Bobby-Boy saying, 'Why do I have a bad feeling about this conversation?'

Then: 'Where it's heading.'

DCI Diaper saying, 'Did it never occur to you... Dennis never having his collar felt once, all those years?'

'I did use to wonder.'

'Think about it.'

Bobby-Boy saying, 'Give me none of that.'

Then: 'Dennis?'

'Who *can* you trust, right?'

'Bollock off.'

'Just so as you know... there is a vacancy.'

Bobby-Boy holding up his empty tumbler, 'Time I got myself a refill.'

DCI Diaper saying, 'You're not that smart, Bobby-Boy.'

'Saving me for a rainy day, were you?'

'If I say Winston Capaldi?'

'Who?'

'Eric Holtz?'

'I read about that... nasty business.'

'Clarice Cliff?'

'Short and curly time, right?'

'Your call, Bobby-Boy.'

Then: 'Cab driver has our man picked up outside Club 67,

around 2.30, afternoon of Eric's murder. Couldn't miss him…
tattoos, body jewellery, leathers, motorcycle security chain
around his neck, Mohican hair-do.'

'Mohawkan… not Mohican.'

'You know him?'

'Not ringing any bells, no.'

'Honour among thieves, right?'

Bobby-Boy saying, 'Honour among thieves?'

Then: 'You must be fucking joking.'

9

Robert saying to Yvonne, 'Will you marry me?'

Yvonne saying, 'How many girls have you been with, Robert?'

'Been with?'

'Slept with… am I the first?'

'What makes you think that?'

'How many?'

'The second.'

'What happened to the first one… she turn you down?'

'I didn't ask her.'

Didn't get the chance… Winston standing there in the
bedroom doorway going on about Bobby-Boy's score – The
Fender Telecaster – Aurelie saying, 'Get the fuck out of my bed.'
Bandage, gauze and tape off Robert's face only yesterday, thanks
a lot, Winston… Yvonne, now, saying, 'You don't have to
propose to a girl every time she wants a fuck.'

'She?'

'Girls like it, too, you know.'

'I don't like it—'

'Could have fooled me.'

'No… you talking that way.'

'What way?'

'It's embarrassing.'

'You mean, we can do it, but we can't talk about it?'

Then: 'Don't go confusing me with your mother, Robert.'

Then: 'Where is he hiding?'

'Who?'

'Your saving grace.'

Reaching beneath the duvet cover, taking Robert in both hands.

Robert saying, 'Oh, Christ! What's the time?'

Then: 'I have to be in Gunnersbury by ten.'

Yvonne saying, 'Gunnersbury?'

'Important match.'

Then: 'Cup game... we're playing last year's runners-up.'

Then: 'Want to come and watch?'

Robert, out of bed, searching for his jeans, black fleece top, Nikes... Yvonne saying, 'Let me get this straight... you're leaving me to go play a game of football?'

Robert, puzzled, couldn't see a problem, saying, 'It's Sunday.'

Thinking, What else do you do on a Sunday?

Yvonne saying, 'The answer is no.'

Robert already forgotten the question.

Other titles by John B Spencer

Tooth & Nail Bloodlines
ISBN 1 899344 31 4 — C-format paperback original, £7
When it comes to property, Reggie Crystal and Terry Reece-Morgan have half of West London carved up between them. But both men have problems: Reggie's is that he likes to swing by the neck from light fittings, while Terry has a wife who is in intensive care — and he can't wait to pull the plug.

A dark, Rackmanesque tale of avarice and malice-aforethought from one of Britain's most exciting and accomplished writers. "Spencer offers yet another demonstration that our crime writers can hold their own with the best of their American counterparts when it comes to snappy dialogue and criminal energy. Recommended." — Time Out

Perhaps She'll Die! Bloodlines
ISBN 1 899344 14 4 — C-format paperback original, £5.99
Giles could never say 'no' to a woman… any woman. But when he tangled with Celeste, he made a mistake… A bad mistake.
Celeste was married to Harry, and Harry walked a dark side of the street that Giles — with his comfortable lifestyle and fashionable media job — could only imagine in his worst nightmares. And when Harry got involved in nightmares, people had a habit of getting hurt. Set against the boom and gloom of eighties Britain, Perhaps She'll Die! is classic noir with a centre as hard as toughened diamond.

Quake City Bloodlines
ISBN 1 899344 14 4 — C-format paperback original, £5.99
Charley Case is the hard-boiled investigator of the near future. But of a future that follows the 'Big One' — The quake that literally rips California apart and makes LA an island. A future where 'cred' status is everything and without it, you're a big fat zero.

It begins when Charley is offered a simple job…

Apartment sitting.

Easy…? But before he's finished, Charley will have been embroiled in sudden unexpected violence, a trail of blood that leads directly to the steps of the Oval Office, and more sudden death than a popular abattoir sees in a wet Los Angeleno fortnight.

The Do-Not Press
Fiercely Independent Publishing

Keep in touch with what's happening at the cutting edge of independent British publishing.

Join The Do-Not Press Information Service and receive advance information of all our new titles, as well as news of events and launches in your area, and the occasional free gift and special offer.

Simply send your name and address to:
The Do-Not Press (Dept. ST)
16 The Woodlands
London
SE13 6TY
or email us: thedonotpress@zoo.co.uk

There is no obligation to purchase and no sales-person will call.

Visit our regularly-updated web site:

http://www.thedonotpress.co.uk

Mail Order
All our titles are available from good bookshops, or (in case of difficulty) direct from The Do-Not Press at the address above. There is no charge for post and packing.
(NB: A post-person may call.)